Other Books by William Post

WILLIAM POST

LOST IN INDIAN COUNTRY

authorHOUSE®

AuthorHouse™
1663 Liberty Drive
Bloomington, IN 47403
www.authorhouse.com
Phone: 1 (800) 839-8640

Published by AuthorHouse 07/17/2017

ISBN: 978-1-5462-0057-4 (sc)
ISBN: 978-1-5462-0056-7 (e)

Print information available on the last page.

Any people depicted in stock imagery provided by Thinkstock are models, and such images are being used for illustrative purposes only. Certain stock imagery © Thinkstock.

This book is printed on acid-free paper.

Because of the dynamic nature of the Internet, any web addresses or links contained in this book may have changed since publication and may no longer be valid. The views expressed in this work are solely those of the author and do not necessarily reflect the views of the publisher, and the publisher hereby disclaims any responsibility for them.

CONTENTS

PREFACE

This is a story about another person caught in the West in the 1860s, trying to survive. Much of life is luck, I believe. When I was discharged from the U. S. Navy, my folks were living in El Paso, Texas. I didn't know a person in that city. I just happened to ask my mother if she knew any cute girls. She told me she knew a checker at a Food Mart. So, I went with her the next time she went for groceries. That was well over fifty years ago, and I hear that checker making dinner right now.

Luck or destiny, who knows. In the old West, luck had a lot to do with it, but learning the ways of the Indians also played a great role in whether a man lived or died. Knowing the terrain, figuring out what an Indian would do, being able to shoot straight, all were important.

Why men insisted on going west into a hostile environment is a question that can be answered only by those who went. It was the longing to own a piece of land, or not having to answer to anyone. It took a brave person to face the West and survive. Many didn't. The Indians were intolerant of the white men taking their land and hunting grounds.

The Indians way of life was one of war. From birth they were taught that a stranger was an enemy. They lived in small tribes and warred among themselves, endlessly. Some historians believe that if the white man had not come to America, they would still be warring on one another with the same weapons. They had no horses until the Spanish came, so this meant they couldn't travel far.

They had to live in small tribes as they needed game to survive and large numbers could not be fed unless they followed the buffalo.

They may be friendly with another tribe for a few years, but that never lasted as feuds developed over petty things.

During the Civil War, the white men left them alone, mostly, but after the Civil War, the Indians were put on reservations. This was because a plan carried out that took away their food supply by killing off the buffalo. Without food, they had to go to the reservations. Their horses were also killed off, so being immobile and not having the buffalo for food, they were forced onto the reservations.

`Pockets of renegade Indians still roamed the West after the Civil War, but they, too, were brought to an end by the late1880s. Every treaty ever made with the Indians was broken by the white man. Greed and hate caused the treaties to be broken.

This story starts during the Civil War and demonstrates the luck and perseverance of an Indian woman and a soldier who by sheer luck, survived an Indian ambush. The woman needed the soldier and he needed her as he was badly wounded. Together they survived.

CHAPTER 1

AMBUSHED

ALVIN SCOTT WAS BEING dragged by an Indian woman. He called to her and she stopped. She then helped him to his feet. She kept her shoulder under his arm pit and helped him walk. It was a long walk, and he had to rest many times. The way was up a mountain, and it was nearly dark when they reached a cave the woman was living in. She laid him on a blanket, and with sign language she was able to tell him she was going back for his rifle. When he was shot, his rifle had fallen under him so the Indians didn't know it was there.

The bugler for the army patrol was the only one who saw the Indians coming, and fell from his horse into a small gully. He made his way to a point about two hundred yards away. He had taken his bugle and had a plan in mind. He could still hear gunshots, so he sounded the cavalry charge. He did it three times. The firing stopped and he could hear the Indians riding away. He went back and viewed where his patrol laid. All were on the ground. He knew the only way to save some of the men, was to return to the temporary fort and get help. He had no horse, so he ran awhile then walked awhile.

Alvin was in the ambushed patrol. He had been shot and fell from his horse with his rifle still in his hands. However, when he hit the ground, everything went black. He awoke while being dragged by an Indian woman.

When they arrived at the cave the woman said, "I go get rifle," and left Alvin on a mat she made for him. He felt his head as it hurt terribly. He then found he had been scalped. They had taken the front of his hair, as they thought he was dead. The Indian scalping Alvin heard the bugle sound just as he started to scalp Alvin, so he took just the front of his scalp and ran to his horse.

Alvin was shot in the shoulder and the bullet had passed through him. It must have cut a vein, because he was drenched in blood. He barely remembered the fight. They were a patrol sent out to scout a tribe of Ute Indians. The Indians had burned several farms and killed everyone. The patrol was ambushed, and they didn't have a chance. The Indians were well armed, and Alvin couldn't remember any of his patrol getting off a shot. His shoulder wound was all that saved his life, as they thought he was dead. They didn't strip any of them as they generally did, because they heard the sound of a bugle. They had heard this sound many times before. It meant certain death if they lingered. They took the horses and what firearms they could see and were gone. They just knew the army was about to come in force.

Alvin had worn two bandoleers, all filled with bullets. He put them under his shirt before he left camp. He had heard of soldiers being killed because they ran out of ammunition. That certainly wasn't going to happen to him, thus the two bandoleers. He thought this a good omen as he never had done that before. He, or now they, had a good supply of bullets.

The Indian woman had witnessed the ambush. She was hiding in the niche of a rock, high up, and could see the Indians set for an ambush. She had seen the bugler go into the ditch and leave. When she heard the sound of his bugle, she knew he was trying to make the Indians think it was the main troop coming.

She smiled as she saw the Indians leaving in a hurry. She stayed where she was and saw the bugler come back and witness the scene. He then turned and ran. After he left, she came down to scavenger anything of use. She came to Alvin and heard him groan. Immediately, she knew he would be of help to her survival, if she could get him to her cave and save him. When she rolled him over, she saw the rifle that would be essential in shooting meat that she desperately needed.

She had been turned out from her tribe because she was caught making love to a warrior whose squaw had great influence. She had then been ostracized by the tribe. In their tradition, they cut her nose to show she was sexually immoral.

When the woman returned, she had Alvin's rifle, a bedroll and saddlebags. She had taken the bedroll and saddlebags from a wounded horse that ran away. The horse had died in a gully that was in their path on the way to the woman's cave.

She built a fire, then removed his shirt. Alvin could see the hole the bullet had made and felt the sting of where the bullet passed out his back. She put a piece of wood in his mouth to bite on. Alvin could see that she had a red hot knife in her hands. He knew she was going to cauterize the wounds on his shoulder and back. It had to be done, but he really dreaded it.

As she seared the wound on his shoulder, it created such pain, that he passed out again. When Alvin awoke, it was morning. His wounds hurt terribly and the pain was so severe that he forgot about his scalped head. She had put some kind of salve on his wounds, that she later told him was from a plant. She had an iron pot that she had salvaged from the saddlebags and had some jerked meat boiling to make a broth. She fed the broth to him around noon. It tasted wonderful, as he had not eaten for nearly twenty-four hours.

Alvin rested during the days, just surviving on broth and some of the jerked meat. Unbeknown to him, the woman had returned to the horse and butchered some of it. She smoked the meat to cure it. However, they ate off a large roast for several days.

Alvin laid on his back taking stock of what he must do when he was well enough to get around. He noticed that the smoke from the fire was carried back into the cave and could not be seen or smelled because of that. There was a constant drip from a place in the top of the cave. The drip went into an olla that the woman must have found someplace. It held over a gallon and the drip was fast enough to furnish them with all the water they needed.

After three days, Alvin had enough strength to stand and move some. They sat opposite of one another and tried to communicate. She knew several English words and Alvin knew some of the Ute language. She said her name was Acula and Alvin told her his name was Alvin. He decided not to burden her with his full name. She was able to communicate that she had been kicked out of her tribe. Alvin knew about the split nose, but didn't say anything about it.

She always slept with him with her arm across his chest and her face on his good shoulder. This was partially because they only had two blankets. She was warm and felt good. Alvin had never slept with a woman, but in his condition he was not bothered with fleshly desires, and to be truthful, she was a squaw and Alvin had a prejudice toward Indians.

As they stayed together for over a week, his prejudice left as he saw her as a caring woman who had saved his life. Although, not given to speaking much, Acula wanted to be able to communicate with him, so they spent hours learning each others language. After a week they could talk, using half English and half Ute.

The second week Alvin was strong enough to hunt. Acula went with him, and he was able to shoot a rabbit. It wasn't what they wanted, but at least they would have meat for supper. When he shot the rabbit, Acula smiled at him, acknowledging his skill.

They stayed three weeks in that cave and Alvin regained much of his strength. Unknown to him, the army had received orders to return to the East. The Army was now needing every troop they could muster, so Alvin's company had been called back to join in the war.

Alvin told Acula that he had to return to the fort. She understood that it was his duty. She didn't like it, but knew she couldn't keep him. She left with him. Alvin knew she needed him, so he didn't say anything about her coming along. He thought that when they reached the fort, the army would send her to a reservation.

They traveled to the army's temporary fort and found it deserted. Alvin found graves with white crosses on them. A cross was put for every member of the patrol, including him. There names were neatly printed on the crosses. He figured they just buried the bodies in a mass grave where they found them, then put up crosses at the fort to acknowledge their deaths.

Alvin thought about what he should do. He had no idea where his troop had gone. They were miles away from any army installation. He had no horse and was still weak from his wounds. He decided to stay with the woman, until they were both in a more tenable position.

They were able to find four blankets and a sack of flour in a store house that were overlooked. The flour had weevils all through it, but they were elated with their find. They also found a rusty skillet, two metal plates, several rusty cups and some eating utensils. They put all of it in a broken backpack that Alvin was able to repair. Acula carried the backpack, and Alvin only carried his rifle. A day later, they were at the cave again.

Alvin took the skillet, plates and cups to a stream. Using sand, he was able to remove all the rust. They now had something to eat and drink with. He commented to Acula that they were beginning to have a good tepee. She smiled.

He killed a doe that week. The minute they arrived at the dead doe, Acula used her knife and cut into the stomach cavity and removed the liver that was still warm. She cut it in half and handed Alvin his portion. He thought, "*What the heck,*" and tried it. To his surprise he liked it. He thought to himself, "*If I am to live like an Indian, I might as well learn to eat like one.*"

They were able to gut the deer and skin it with a knife that Acula had acquired from a dead soldier. She knew exactly how to butcher the deer. She cut the meat in small strips and smoked them on racks she had made from a willow tree. They now had enough jerky to last them a couple of weeks or more.

They lived in the cave for several weeks mainly because a snow storm had blown through and covered everything with a foot of snow. The snow did not melt for two weeks. When it was nearly gone, Acula said, "We go." She indicated that she had a better place for them. So they packed everything they had in two backpacks.

Alvin had made another backpack out of the deer skin. They walked for several days around a mountain. They walked slowly and were hypersensitive to the possibilities of Indians being in the area. Every so often, Acula would raise her hand and Alvin knew he was to stop and be quiet. He began to distinguish sounds of the wilds. He knew that if the birds failed to sing and everything went deathly quiet, that he must be perfectly still and hide. He knew if he were caught again, that it would be a slow, painful death.

They started up the side of a mountain that was very steep for awhile, then leveled off. They were ultra quiet when they traveled never talking, only using sign language. Alvin knew he had very little training in the wilds, and that Acula was born to them.

Acula was also aware that if the Ute warriors caught them, they would kill Alvin and do worse to her. Just as she was thinking this, they heard voices. They were far away, but they faintly heard them.

They found a hiding place under a rock overhang that kept them hidden. They gathered pine needles for their bed and stayed there two day until they felt the Indians were long gone. During that time, they made no fires. A stream was nearby and at night they would go to it for water. Alvin was very scared and relied on Acula for everything.

At one point they were confronted by a mother bear. They gave her a wide berth, as they both knew what would happened if she came for them. Alvin would have loved to have the lard from the bear, but he would not chance the noise being heard from his rifle by the Indians. Besides the two cubs would be without a mother and probably die.

As Alvin walked he thought of what he must do. He knew he was in Indian country and that he probably wouldn't last a week without the woman. He laughed to himself as he realized she felt the same way. They were an odd couple, but needed one another for survival. He thought that he must learn the ways of the Indian, if he were to survive.

Acula was a good teacher, and he listened to every word she said, which were few. He learned the most from her actions.

CHAPTER 2

THE CABIN

After another week of travel, they came to a fast water stream that ran against a six or seven hundred-foot cliff. The cliff ran for over a mile. Over centuries the stream must have carved out the bottom of the cliff as it now overhung the stream.

An area bulged out from the cliff, leaving a place where the stream ran around it for five or six hundred feet. Alvin thought this was from the top of the cliff breaking off eons ago. The place was raised and was a flat shelf of about 30 to 60 feet wide against the cliff, then sloped back to the creek. Alvin only knew this later as the entire bulge was densely covered with fir trees, ferns and vines.

They crossed the stream at the west end of the bulge and it appeared that Acula was taking them into a sheer cliff, until Alvin noticed a huge rock that sat about three or four feet from the wall of the cliff. There, she turned and went between the cliff and the rock. It was an entrance to a steep path, which took them through the fir trees to the top of the shelf. The water of the stream was ice cold and Alvin was very glad to be out of it.

A hundred feet along the path, they came to a clearing that contained a cabin. It was built nearly against the cliff with trees in front of it that hid it from anyplace across the creek. They entered the cabin and Alvin noticed the door had iron hinges on it and fit tightly to the sill.

After Acula opened some shutters, he noticed that the cabin was illuminated by three windows, one on each wall, except the back which had a door. Alvin was curious, as he knew that the cabin sat nearly against the cliff, so he opened the door. It led into a horizontal mine shaft that contained coal. He marveled that the cabin had an endless supply of fuel.

After Acula opened the shutters of the windows, Alvin's eyes wandered about. There was a table with four chairs and a stone fireplace, that had an iron grill for cooking. In front of the fireplace was a wooden sofa that was padded by a bearskin. Several bearskins were on the floor. The cabin was about sixteen by twenty feet in area and ten feet in height at the highest point of the roof. There was a loft for sleeping, as to add more floor space for living. In one corner was a walled in toilet with a large chamber pot under the seat to catch the waste.

Acula later showed Alvin that the chamber pot was to be emptied in a place away from the house to dry. She would sprinkle it with a white powder that Alvin knew was lime, so there were no flies. Every week or so, she would distribute the dried waste in an area used for a garden that was about thirty by fifty feet. The garden appeared to be blooming with several plants. He later learned that potatoes, yams, beets and onions were a winter crop and that come spring the garden would also have squash, corn, beans, sugarcane and other vegetables.

Alvin was amazed at the precision that everything had been constructed. The logs fit tightly together and had been caulked both front and back with adobe mud mixed with straw. The floor was made of slate that fit tightly together. There were shelves for food staples and a row of about thirty books. There was even a jug of whiskey.

Acula hummed as she prepared dinner. Alvin could tell she was very happy to be home. He sat down on the sofa as he was very tired from the day's walk. He poured himself a snort of whisky from the jug and was very happy.

Alvin thought about his troop. It had probably been called back to aid in the war effort. The Indians could wait until after the war. If he were with his troop, it probably wouldn't be long until he was killed. As they thought he was dead, no one would be the wiser. He would just wait out the war with Acula.

Acula had dug some potatoes and onions to go with the rabbit Alvin had killed along the way. He noticed that she carefully dug out the eyes of the potatoes and planted them in a wooded tray to sprout. Outside, between the cabin and the garden, was a shack used to house tools. There was nearly every tool anyone would want, plus a grinding wheel to sharpen any tool that needed it. Whoever had built this cabin was a skilled man.

That night after supper, Acula told Alvin the history of the cabin. She said a man, named Thomas (the only name Acula knew), had built the cabin some fifteen years ago. After he had it like he wanted it, he went to a rendezvous that was held at the base of the Rocky Mountains most years.

Thomas won two mules in a poker game and traded the mules to Acula's father for her. At first Acula was sad, as she knew she would be leaving her mother and her brothers and sisters. However, she was obedient and went with Thomas.

He spoke her dialect like a native, and they always spoke in her tongue. He was an older man past his forties, but very strong. He took her to the cabin, which she immediately adored. It made living so much easier.

Thomas was good to Acula and she had never known a man to treat a woman so nice. He gave her time to get to know him before he made love to her. He took time showing her the nuances of love making, as he thought of her pleasure above his. She began to love him.

They lived together four years in the cabin. She never became pregnant although they made love very often. Thomas pleased her in many ways and showed her how to please him.

One day, Thomas went hunting. After two days, where he failed to return, Acula went to find him. She was able to trace his footsteps and after several hours came upon his body. He had been scalped and stripped of his clothing. Just a nude corpse was left.

Thomas had taught Acula to always take a coil of rope, her hatchet and knife when traveling. She cut some limbs and made a travois to drag him home. When she arrived, she used a shovel and dug a grave by the cabin. She tied a cross together and put it at the head of the grave.

Thomas was a Christian and had explained the love of Jesus to Acula. She didn't understand it all, but she knew that the great spirit had a son, called Jesus, and had been sent to the world in human form, to take away the sins of the people by shedding his blood, while dying on a cross. He had then risen from the dead and ascended into heaven with his tribe watching him rise. He had promised eternal life for those who believed in him. If Thomas believed in Jesus, Acula certainly would. She knew Thomas would want a cross at the head of his grave and she asked the great spirit to take Thomas to the Jesus he loved.

Alvin and Acula settled into a good life. They had all they needed and were kept busy keeping it that way. Acula taught Alvin many things. They decided to speak Ute one day and English the next. That way, they would learn both languages. Alvin worked on Acula's diction and little by little she began to lose her accent. Acula also worked on Alvin's diction and he too, began to lose his accent.

Acula noticed how Alvin always asked her opinion about anything they were going to do. She liked this, and it made her love Alvin all the more.

Acula was raised in a Ute tribe. Her grandfather was a white man. Because of this, her hair was not jet black like the others, but dark brown. Her eyes were also brown, unlike all the others whose eyes were black. She was comely, which caused several braves to want her. However, her father knew about the rendezvous and figured he could trade both his daughters for horses.

After Thomas' death, Acula lived alone for nearly a year, but she became very lonely and decided to return to the tribe. Her father was now dead and her mother had been taken by another warrior who had lost his wife. They lived close to a warrior whose wife had become fat and ugly. However, the woman's father was the chief of the tribe, and she had great influence with him.

Acula noticed the woman's husband looking at her a lot. She kept her distance from him, but one day she was alone in her tepee. The warrior appeared and he began to rape her. His squaw heard the commotion and peered into the tent and saw the warrior making love to Acula. The squaw went to her father and Acula was branded an outcast. The squaw had two of her brothers hold Acula while she cut her nosed. She was given nothing but the clothes on her back, and told to leave the tribe and never come back.

After a week of walking, she found the cave. Someone had lived there before and she found several things, such as a hatchet and an olla, that saved her life. Thomas had shown her how to make snares for small animals, and she existed like that for three weeks.

She was about to return to the cabin when she saw the army patrol being ambushed by the Ute tribe. She waited until the war party left, then sneaked about the bodies trying to find something of use. She did. She found Alvin Scott.

Although Alvin loved Acula, he was not in love with her. He knew eventually he would want to return to civilization. The problem was, he knew Acula was very much in love with him. He had a tender heart and just couldn't leave her high and dry.

After what happened to Thomas, Acula would never let Alvin hunt alone. She was within fifty feet of him at all times. Alvin understood this was because she had lost Thomas by not being with him when he was killed.

Alvin went for water each day. They had a path in front of the cabin that descended to the creek. It wound around some so that a path could not be seen from across the creek. One morning Scott wanted to bring back some sand and gravel from the creek, as some of the iron trays had become rusty and he wanted to clean the rust off them.

As Scott was scooping out the sand and gravel he noticed some of the pebbles were gold nuggets. He knew the difference from iron pyrite and gold, and this was definitely gold. He was now excited. He went back to the cabin and got a steel wash basin and returned with it to the creek. He used the wash basin as a gold pan and began swirling the sand and gravel around. Gold was in every pan. He would dump the gold into the pail he had with him. He worked all morning.

Near noon, Acula came down to the creek and asked what he was doing. He took a break as he was hungry. They went back to the cabin and Alvin showed her the gold. He explained that the white men valued gold above anything, and they could buy anything they wanted if they had enough of it.

Acula loved to do new things, and she began to use one of the steel trays and became very adept at panning gold. They worked half a day panning, as the rest of the day was needed to garden, spread their fertilizer and do various things around the house.

They began wandering up and down the creek panning and found a place near the east end, where the creek started around the bulge. This area was rich in gold. It was located where the creek met the cliff again.

Scott examined the wall of the cliff and could see just below the waterline, a seam of milky quartz where gold went through it like a spider web. He knew he could chisel the gold out of it if he wanted. However, the gold in the stream was easier to get, so they continued to pan.

As Alvin panned, he thought of what would happen if anyone found out about the gold. Thousands of people would descend on them. He knew that they must be very careful to conceal their find.

Each night, Alvin would melt what gold they had panned in an iron pot and pour it into a mold he had made out of clay. The gold from the mold was a small rectangle that contain enough gold to weigh about five pounds. They panned the whole summer and late into the fall. They now had nine, five-pound ingots.

Before it snowed Alvin said, "Acula, do you know of the whiteman's village to the east? It's called Denver.

Acula said, "I have heard of it. Many white people live there."

Are there Indians between here and the village?"

Acula shook her head, but she didn't like where this was going as she knew that Alvin was thinking of going to the white eyes' village and may leave her.

Alvin saw the look on her face and immediately knew what she was thinking. He said, "I will not leave you Acula, I promise."

Acula then said, "I don't think the Ute tribe is in that area, but the Arapaho are. However, they are friendly to the white eyes."

Alvin then said, "I want us to go to Denver. We have need of several items, such as clothes, salt, sugar and several other items. I could buy chickens and goats that would make our life easier."

Acula then believed Alvin would return as he would be bringing chickens and goats. They then began planning their trip. They would take two backpacks with two ingots of gold in each pack.

Acula didn't want to go where white people were, but Alvin said, "I'll dress you up like a white woman and I'll bet no one will know you're Indian."

Acula was apprehensive, but if Alvin wanted this, then that is what she would do.

CHAPTER 3

DENVER

Their trip to Denver was uneventful. They saw Indians along the way, but no one bothered them. After they reached Denver, Alvin asked a man on the street where they could sell gold. The man asked, "How much do you have?"

Alvin said, "Several pounds."

The man whistled and said, "The mint buys gold in large quantities. I'd try there. It's just down the block and has a large sign. You can't miss it."

Alvin knew they were crudely dressed and he hadn't shaved in sometime. However, they entered the mint and a clerk came to them with a smile. He asked, "How may I help you?"

Without saying anything, Alvin laid the four ingots on the counter. The clerk picked one of the ingots up and said, "This looks nearly pure. I take it, you would like a price?" and Alvin nodded.

The clerk said, "We are in need of gold and after we assay it, we can give you a price."

Alvin was embarrassed, but then said, "Could you give us an advance. We have just come from the mountains and need to clean up and buy some clothes and get a room."

The clerk said, "I can advance you a hundred dollars, will that be enough?"

Alvin smiled and said, "Yes, thank you." He then asked, "Is there some place that we could bathe and get our hair cut?"

The clerk said, "Across the street and several doors down, you will find a barbershop that will take care of all you needs."

After getting a receipt from the clerk, Scott thanked the man and took the hundred dollars. On the way to the barbershop, they came to a clothing store for men and women. They entered and Scott picked out two dresses for Acula, along with underwear shoes and socks. He bought himself a suit, a pair of slacks, a hat, underwear, boots and socks. They then went on to the barbershop.

They were shown to a back room that contained a large tub, big enough for both of them. It had hot water and soap for them. They spent a half-hour in the tub then dried and put on their clothes. They both looked good, except for their hair. Alvin's beard was now about two inches. He had a shave and a haircut and the barber was very good at cutting Acula's hair and putting some curls in it with hot iron rollers.

Acula couldn't believe the difference in herself. She looked similar to the white women she had seen on the street. Alvin looked so handsome that she just marveled at him. While paying the barber, he asked the barber if he would sell him a razor, shaving soap, some scissors and some curling irons, which he did.

They went to a hotel and registered as Mr. and Mrs. Alvin Scott. They were shown to a room that was more elegant that either had ever seen. Acula said, "We must speak only English, and help me if I blunder."

They went to the dining room to eat and Alvin told Acula to just eat like he did. She watched carefully and did as he did. They had ordered steak and it was delicious. After dinner they had a slice of apple pie. Acula said, "I must learn to make pies. Thomas told me about them, but this is the first I have ever eaten. It is delicious. After dinner they walked the streets looking at the tall buildings. They passed by a confectionary and Alvin bought her some chocolates. She was amazed at the wonderful taste.

Alvin had never smoked, but he had seen others smoke, so he bought a cigar. After lighting it and taking a couple of puffs, he handed it to Acula, who took a couple of puffs and spit, while handing it back to Alvin. Alvin said, "I feel the same way," and threw it away.

They went to bed early, then went to the hotel dining room and had a hearty breakfast of flap-jacks, beacon and eggs. Acula said, I must learn to cook flapjacks."

Alvin said, "I can teach you that. Even I know how to do that."

They then went to the mint and the clerk didn't recognize them. Alvin laughed and showed him the receipt. The clerk looked closer and said, "I am completely awed at the change in your appearances. My, you are a handsome couple. How long have you been married?"

Alvin said, "Nearly five years now." This made Acula smile as she understood all what was being said.

The assay had been completed and the clerk gave them a price of forty-eight hundred dollars, which Alvin agreed.

The clerk asked, "Will you be bringing us some more ingots Mr. Scott?"

"Yes, if we can find some more gold. This took us a long time to accumulate, so it might be some time before we see you again."

The clerk said, "We like your gold, as it is easy to work with. I hope to see you every season."

Alvin asked the clerk, "Do you know a doctor?"

The clerk said, "There is a new doctor who works out of his house. He surely needs the business, as he is new and doesn't have many customers yet. I like him and he knows all the newest procedures." They were directed down the block to a Dr. Forbes. Acula had no idea why they would go to a doctor, but if that was what Alvin wanted, she would go along.

Dr. Forbes was a young doctor fresh from the East, and being he had few patients, he welcomed them with a smile. He asked, "How may I help you?"

Alvin said, "My wife was cut on the nose and I was wondering if you can mend it."

Forbes examined it and said, "I think I can fix it. It will be painful, as I must cut both sides then sew it together. In a few weeks it will grow back together. I don't think it will leave much of a scar"

Listening to this Acula wanted this badly. The doctor had nothing to deaden her nose, so he gave her some alcohol to drink. Alvin held her hands as the doctor cut her. She didn't make a sound, but squeezed Alvin's hands very tightly. Tears poured from her eyes and she noticed that tears were pouring from Alvin's eyes as well. She loved him more at that instant than at anytime they had known one another, because she knew he loved her.

When doctor Forbes was through sewing her up he said, "The love I saw between you two made me weep as well. I feel I love you both, now."

Alvin shook Dr. Forbes' hand and said, "How much do I owe you, Doctor?"

"One dollar. You must come back in a week and I will remove the stitches."

"We will be in the mountains by then, Doctor. I will remove them with my pin knife."

"Knowing the love between you two, I don't need to tell you to be careful."

After they left the doctor's office Acula said, "You told the clerk at the mint that we were married five years. When did we get married?"

"When you saved my life and took me in. I counted each month as a year that we were married."

She smiled at him and said, "I do too. I loved Thomas, but never like I love you. Jesus gave you to me, I just know."

"Maybe he did." They walked further and Alvin said, "Lets shop around for a wagon. We need to buy a couple of goats and some chickens. I surely want to buy a couple of Sharps repeating rifles and two handguns. They bought enough ammunition to hold off an army. Alvin said, "I want to teach you to shoot. Two people can hold off a great number, if both are firing repeating rifles."

They bought two mules and a wagon. They outfitted it to carry two goats and six chickens. They bought a roll of chicken wire, along with a roll of bailing wire, a hundred feet of rope, twenty pounds of sugar, ten pounds of salt, twenty pounds of coffee, fifty pounds of flour, a case of whiskey, and many seeds for their garden. They also bought along several tools to add to the ones in their shed. That included a keg of nails and a cross-cut saw.

They drove only a mile or two out of Denver and Scott stopped and said, "I think this is the place for you to learn to shoot. I will set up a target by that bluff and teach you."

Alvin began with the safety features of his rifle. He then taught her to aim and squeeze the trigger. She learned slowly, but Alvin was convinced that she would improve over time. He had seen other females who couldn't do much of anything like shooting. However, Acula was more like a man in those areas, as she had worked hard all her life. He then handed her a thirty-eight Colt revolver. She seemed to be better with a pistol than the rifle. They practiced several hours, then made camp and left the next morning.

It took five days to reach the place where they crossed the creek. The distance wasn't that far, but the mountainous terrain was hard to traverse. They had made better time hiking.

They were very wary of Indians and held to the trees as much as they could. They never saw an Indian or even a trace of them.

Arriving at the west end of the creek they unloaded everything. Alvin drove the wagon and the mules to a place about a hundred feet away, where there was a small glade within the trees. He would put the mules on a rope, long enough so they could reach the water and still crop grass. The glade was hidden and far enough off the trail so the mules could not be seen or heard. It took another day to get the chickens and goats to a place on the west side of the cabin and make pens for both of them.

A week later Alvin cut the sutures very carefully and pulled out the stitches. Dr. Forbes had given Alvin some aloe vera to apply to Acula's nose, which he did religiously each day.

Alvin built a coop for the hens and made nests for them. Acula helped in every endeavor Alvin took on. They loved to work together. Acula was so handy that they seldom talked, as she could see the things Alvin needed, and would get them for him. She loved to learn about everything.

The hens now produced an egg everyday. They didn't eat any of the eggs as they wanted them to hatch and increase their number. They were awaken each dawn with the rooster crowing.

Alvin built a shelter for the goats. Each day Alvin hiked down and tended to the mules. He began building them a corral that went to the creek. Acula was with him all day and helped in everything he did. As the water was very swift at that point, the mules never went into the water. He built a shelter for them as he knew the winter could get quite raw. He had bought a scythe and knew where a patch of Timothy hay was. They worked very hard baling many bundles and were able to create a haystack. He put a tarp, he found in his shed to cover most of the haystack. They battened it down with ropes and many stakes. as they knew the winds could get high. However, the cliff shielded the north wind from them as well as much of the snow they knew would come.

That winter they had a lot of time on their hands, so Alvin began teaching Acula to read. She first learned the alphabet and how to pronounce the letters, then he showed her how the letters came together to make words, then how the words made a sentence. To keep this from becoming monotonous, Alvin taught her arithmetic. She was fascinated with the numbers. Acula never tired from learning, although Alvin did at times. She liked it because Alvin was close to her.

Acula had never loved like this before. She simply adored Alvin. He was so thoughtful and loved to please her. She in turn loved him dearly. When they made love she thought it was the most wonderful thing in the world to please him.

Alvin read books to her and she followed along as best she could. She was fascinated with the stories. Her father and mother had told their children stories, but they were not like the books. Defoe's *Robinson Crusoe* was especially good. It was hard for her to image other countries, so Alvin made a list of things they would want in Denver. Alvin wanted a globe of the world, so he could teach Acula geography. They had pen and paper and Alvin tried to show her, but she just couldn't imagine the world.

Alvin really enjoyed teaching Acula, as he would see her eyes as they drank in his every word. Alvin had a little musical training in high school and he tried to teach her the notes by drawing the musical clefs. She got this pretty good and could follow Alvin when he sang the notes. He had hoped to take her to a concert in Denver if they had an orchestra. He thought he would watch Acula more than the orchestra if he had the opportunity.

They talked about children, but Acula couldn't get pregnant. Alvin thought, *"I wouldn't have time for the children as I have Acula to educate."*

Alvin began to fall in love. He had never been in love and it was a new experience to him. They prayed every night, as Thomas had taught her to pray. She began to understand the meaning of Jesus more and more and loved to talk about it with Alvin.

Whereas, winter had always been a drudgery to Acula before, she now loved it, as she spent time with Alvin. Once with great apprehension she asked Alvin, "Will we be together in heaven?"

Alvin said, "I'm sure we will, Acula. God would not separate a love like we have for one another."

She then said, "You're right, Alvin, he wouldn't, because he loves us."

That winter Alvin thought it would be safe to use the rifles and they practiced a lot. Acula became much better and was becoming quite accurate. Alvin said, "From now on when we hunt, I want you to cover me. If anyone comes upon me, you will be there to help me. It will give us an added advantage."

Acula asked, "How far apart?" She had a long face and Alvin said, "Not very far," and she smiled.

Alvin applied the aloe vera to Acula's nose and in three months, the scare was completely gone except for four tiny dots where the stitches had been. Alvin thought they too would be gone by the middle of winter. Which they were.

They spent a lot of the day learning each others language. Acula had little accent now and Alvin worked with her constantly.

Alvin had bought a large mirror for Acula. He had also bought her combs and hairbrushes. He had bought the curling irons and spent a lot of time with her hair. She loved the attention and wanted to look beautiful for him. He had bought her a lot of clothes and had made a closet for them to hang them in. They both had thick wool coats where the collars were about eight inches long and could be turned up past their ears. She had several pair of slacks that fit her well. She liked the khaki color the best.

She said, "the khaki color blends in with the forest. With my dark green shirt, I am practically invisible in the woods."

The barber had combed Alvin's hair to the front so his bald scar would not show. Wearing it that way, the hair now just lay to the front by itself. They cut each others hair once a month and Alvin shaved once a week.

They tended the mules everyday. They both liked to go to the corral and bring the mules hay from their haystack. Alvin said, "This spring, I want to build a shack here and make it look like someone lives here. If the Indians were to come, they would just think someone lives here and is away. I was even thinking of hiring a man to live here and tend to the mules.

"We could then spend more time panning gold. I think it may play out soon, then we will have to mine the milky quartz. There's much more gold there than in the stream, but it's much harder work. I haven't figured how we would mine that strata yet, but I will think on it."

Acula said, "Don't we have enough? We still have five ingots."

"You're right. If we mine the gold then others will find out. I think we should take all of our gold to the mint the next time we go to Denver. We could then put the money in the bank and maybe invest it."

"What is invest?" Acula asked.

Alvin said, "Like if we lent money to someone and they paid us interest."

Acula then asked what is interest"

"It is money the person borrowing the money would pay us for its use."

Acula couldn't really understand this, so she just nodded. Acula could now read and Alvin helped her by telling her not to read every word. He said, "Just let your eyes go ahead and read the whole sentence.

Alvin had bought a dictionary and Acula was constantly looking up words. She would ask Alvin first, then look the word up to see if he were accurate.

She was getting the hang of reading and began really enjoying it. They had enough books to last them the winter. Alvin drew out the world as best he could to show it to her. He first started with America and the oceans that surrounded it. She began getting the concept of geography. He showed her the four directions, which she knew in her native language, but really didn't get the concept until she understood the map of America. She was amazed at the size of the oceans and asked if they could see one of them someday.

Alvin said, "I don't see why not. We will have money to travel and I would enjoy taking you to see every ocean that touches America. Of course we will have to wait until that confounded war is over."

CHAPTER 4

THE ABDUCTION

It was turning summer and Acula went to feed the mules, while Alvin was toting water to the cabin. She had just reached the corral, when two Indians jumped her. She didn't want to scream as she knew Alvin would come and they may kill him.

The Indians set fire to the shack and took the mules with ropes. They put Acula on one of the mules and rode away. They went south.

After Alvin had put the water up he went outside and saw the smoke. He went back into the cabin. He thought if Indians had taken Acula he would be in for a long hike. He made up a bedroll, packed a lot of jerky and his canteen in his backpack. He packed his fire-making equipment, put on two bandoliers, strapped on his holster and pistol then picked up his rifle. He thought he might need some money, so he went to their hiding place near where they dried the dung and retrieved six hundred dollars.

He knew if it were Indians, he would be gone a long time. He must first find where they were going, then track them to their camp. He would then have to figure out a way to get Acula back.

The Indians who took Acula were her own tribe. However, she had changed her looks so much that the Indians thought she was a white woman. They had not waited for her man, if she had one, as they wanted to avoid a fight if possible. There could be more than one white men and this could result in a problem.

Alvin found the tracks of the unshod horses and his shod mules. He followed them. They were moving much faster than he was, but he thought, *"No matter, I'll follow them to where their camp is and take my time."*

While in the army, they had come through a settlement called Alamosa. It had good farm land and many German immigrants had come to that area and were raising potatoes. The Indians held to the edge of the mountains and Alvin just followed until they approached the South Pass. Here, Alvin turned east hoping to find the settlement of Alamosa, so he could buy a horse. As he traveled, there were numerous farms and a settlement. He found there were several buildings including a livery stable. They had a hotel, so the first thing Alvin did was to get a room and a bath. He had bought a change of clothes at a general store, before checking into the hotel. So, after his bath, he now felt clean and refreshed.

The hotel had a bar and he thought he might gain some knowledge about the Indians if he went there. He ordered a whiskey, while standing next to a man who resembled the mountain men he had seen when he was first at the fort.

He turned to the man and said, "I'm Alvin Scott, could I buy you a drink?"

The man put a smile on his face and said, "You must be a stranger. No one in this town will have anything to do with me. I'm a mountain man, and they think I'm too crude to be friendly with. My name is Kit Carson. Why are you in town, Mr. Scott?"

"A band of Indians took my two mules and wife three days ago. I set off on foot to get her back."

"Wow, you must love her very much to take on a tribe of Indians."

"That I do, and I want to hire someone who knows the country to help guide me."

"I know nearly every tribe in this area and am looking for work. If the Indians you are following are Comanche, your chances are impossible."

"I am nearly sure they are Ute," Alvin said.

"I've dealt with the Ute. They are a warring people, but they also like to trade. If you have something to trade them, you might just buy back your wife. I'll tell you what I'll do, for fifty dollars, I will go with you and try to buy back your wife."

Alvin reached for his wallet and found two twenty dollar notes and a ten. He laid them in front of Carson. Carson grinned and said, "That lady is very lucky to have a man who loves her that much. If the Indians turn out to be Comanche, then the deal is off, and I will return your money. The Comanche will not deal with a white man, just kill him.

"However, if they are Ute, I will go into their village and try to make a deal. I will tell them I am looking for a white woman and am willing to give two horses for her. The Ute love horses. They will tell me she is worth six horse, but we will finally end up with four. To them, horses are the most valuable things on earth. So if you will buy four horses we will be on our way tomorrow morning."

Alvin said, "Five horses as I am afoot. I also want my mules back."

"I forgot that. Let's go over to the livery stable and talk to Levi. Let me do the haggling. I know his weak points," as he smiled at Alvin.

They left and just like Carson said, they got the horses much cheaper than what Levi first told what there prices were. At the end of the deal Carson went to his saddle bags that were hung up in the stable and pulled out a quart of whiskey and handed it to Levi.

Levi turned to Alvin and with a smile said, "Don't ever trade with this man, or he will end up with your eyeteeth," and they all laughed.

Alvin said, "I'll want the best of the five horses to ride myself. I need a saddle with a rifle sleeve and some saddle bags."

I can sell you a saddle with a rifle sleeve, but lets just the two of us deal, as I don't want to give it away." They all laughed and Alvin paid Levi twenty-five dollars for a very nice saddle. Levi said, "You'll have to get the saddlebags at the general store."

They went to the general store and Alvin bought supplies for the trip plus the saddlebags.

As they were retuning to the hotel Carson said, "I see the Indians took on something they shouldn't, you look very determined."

"Determined I am. The Indians went toward the south pass, but being afoot, I decided to come east to buy a horse and maybe hire a mountain man as a guide."

As they rode, Carson said, "I know of a Ute Village just over the South Pass. We should be there in a couple of days."

Carson always slept near the horses just incase Indians tried to steal them. The Comanche Indians were the best horse stealers in the world. Carson had lost his horse once to one of them and it took him two weeks to catch up with him. He prided himself in stealing the horse back.

They crossed the South Pass and could see the smoke from the Ute Village. They found a stream and a place to hold up for a few days. Carson said that he would go to the Ute village alone and see if they had a white woman for sale. Alvin described Acula and told him to talk to her before he made a trade. She would tell him in English if she were Acula and married to Alvin Scott.

The next day Carson was off. He entered the Ute village with everyone looking at him. He rode up to a large tepee and dismounted. The chief knew him, as he had traded with him before. They sat in the chief's tepee and smoked. Carson didn't say a word. The chief eventually asked, "Why you come to my village, Carson?"

Carson waited awhile then said, "I want to buy a white woman from you."

The chief waited awhile then said, "What would you give me if I had a white woman?"

Carson again waited, then said, "If she is good and can work, I may give you two horses. However, I would have to see her."

The chief said something to one of his wives and she left. Nothing was said until the wife returned with a white woman. She looked like she had been beaten and was lean from not eating.

Carson said, "The woman is not very pretty. Can she work well?"

The chief said, "She works good."

Carson looked at the woman and said, "Do you speak English?"

The woman nodded, so Carson continued and said, "What's your name?"

The woman said, "Acula Scott."

Carson then waved his hand for her to leave. He turned to the chief and said, "She is pretty skinny. Do you think she will live another two or three years?"

The chief said, "If you feed her well, she will last you for years and bear you many sons."

Carson didn't answer for awhile so the chief said, "She is worth many horses."

Carson said, "She doesn't seem like she will live too long. Two horses is all she is worth."

The chief said, "At least five horses."

Carson shook his head then said, "I'll give three horses, but that is all."

The chief sat awhile then said, "Done."

They stood and Carson said, "Send two braves with me. I will give them the horses. You will find that the horses are in much better shape than the woman."

Two braves went with Carson. It took only two hour to get to where Alvin was with the horses. Acula had ridden behind Carson. When they arrived Alvin could see them coming and put himself behind a rock with his rifle, so he would have a clear shot if anything went wrong. When Carson dismounted Alvin could see Acula and his heart jumped with joy.

The Indians slide down and looked at the horses. They picked three of them and were happy as they were good horse. They didn't stay the night and rode off putting some distance between Carson and themselves, as they had heard that Carson was a dangerous mountain man and good at stealing horses.

After the braves left, Carson said, "You can come out now, the Indians are gone."

Alvin walked up behind Acula and she turned and grabbed him. Tears of joy ran down both their faces."

Carson said, "Let's pack up and leave. I want to get at least five miles away from here before we bed down."

They were gone in less than fifteen minutes. It was dark when they camped. Alvin boiled some water with Jerky in it and heated some beans and jerky. Acula was starved. She ate slowly though and not too much. They held each other all night. They left before dawn and made their way back to the town where Alvin had met Carson. Not much talk was made along the trail.

Carson explained that he didn't see the mules in the Indian camp, so he didn't ask for them. He said, "The Indians love mule meat. I'm sure they butchered them, besides I got Acula for just three horses.

Alvin got them a room in the hotel and while she was bathing, bought her some riding clothes and a nice dress for that evening. He also bought her shoes socks and underwear.

At dinner that night Alvin handed Carson another fifty dollars. However, Carson said, "No, I agreed to only fifty and that is all I will accept." He then said, "I will let you buy me dinner, though."

Carson looked at Acula and said, "If that chief could see you now, he would want ten horses."

Acula smiled and said, "I also work good," and they all laughed. She then asked, "How did you two get together?"

Alvin said, "The Lord brought us together. He knew our love and brought me to this town. Carson was standing right next to me. I knew at the time, it was divine intervention. Carson is known as the best mountain man in America."

"I will have to tell you, I am not the best mountain man as I have met Jim Bridger and several others that I couldn't hold a candle to. However, I knew that chief in the Ute village, as I had done some trading with him before. So maybe it was divine intervention."

They were not in a hurry to leave. They took three horses and packed well to make the trip easier. They went straight home as they wanted nothing more than being in their cabin together.

It took four more days as they traveled at a slow, but steady pace. They were again home and everything was in place. They spent the next two weeks building back the shack.

As they were building it, Alvin said, "What do you think about taking on a prospector. We could split all his findings and we wouldn't have to work so hard."

Acula said, "Let me think about that awhile. Now, no one knows about our gold, but if another knows it could get out."

"Yes, I see what you mean. However, if we are selective, we may find someone who would not divulge our secret and make us a lot of money. We are amateurs when it comes to panning. An expert could probably find ten times what we would find. Let's think on it for a few days and then make a decision."

Acula and Alvin loved working together. Once they thought about someone living in the shack, they took more pains with it. They made it much larger and more comfortable. Acula thought that maybe the prospector would want a woman, so she put in things that a woman may want.

Alvin said, "Let's furnish it well, even if we don't bring a prospector. We might want to spend a night or two here ourselves."

Acula rolled her eyes and said, "You are making me want you, when you talk like that."

Alvin said, "I always want you."

It was finally decided to look at a few men and if one looked promising then they would decide then.

CHAPTER 5

A RETURN TO DENVER

It was now turning fall. The liquid ambers and other deciduous trees were turning colors. They both knew it was time to leave before the snow came. They packed up all their gold, and four more ingots they had mined. They were off and it took less time than before, as farming had started and the trail was wider and better due to the wagon traffic. They went to a hotel that they always stayed in, and after cleaning up went to the mint.

The clerk remember them and Alvin handed him the ingots. The clerk wrote them a receipt and as he completed it Alvin asked, "Do you know of any prospectors? We may want to employ one if he has a tight mouth."

The clerk thought a minute and said, "I think I have your man. His name is Jake Magee. He lives on Colton Road on your way out of town toward the mountains. He has a shack there. Anyone can tell you where he lives, if you don't find him right away."

They went directly to Jake's cabin. It was not a shack as the clerk had described. It was well built and well kept. Jake was sitting on a chair outside smoking his pipe when they arrived. There were two more chairs and Jake asked them to sit.

Alvin said, "I asked the clerk at the mint if he knew any prospectors that we could trust. He immediately said your name.

"We have found a creek that has some gold in it. We are novices, but have panned that creek for two years and brought out what we think is a lot of gold. However, we thought if we could do that good, what would a professional prospector do? We don't want anyone knowing where we are getting the gold, for obvious reasons. Would you be interested in coming with us? The deal is, we get half of what you pan and we have a place for you to live and will furnish your food. However, you will have to cook it."

Jake hadn't said anything, but then asked, "How much gold did you bring out?"

"About twenty pounds."

"You mean ounces."

"No, I mean pounds."

Jake whistled and said, "I am beginning to like you two very much. As a matter of fact I think of you as family," and they all smiled.

He then said, "Is it safe from Indians?"

"I can't tell you for sure. We had a little trouble with them last year, as they stole our two mules. However, we found that their tribe is on the other side of South Pass, so I don't look for any trouble."

"Well, I think it is worth the risk. However, it gets mighty lonely out in the wilds. I know a Mexican cook that is sweet on me. Would it be okay for her to come with me? She doesn't even know what I do for a living, and I will see that I keep it that way."

Alvin looked at Acula and she said, "It would be lonely, but with someone else knowing, there is always the danger of word getting out."

Jake said, "I would only show her a little color and tell her the danger of telling anyone about the gold."

"As it is fall, do you want to come with us now or wait until spring?"

"You've got me in a lather, so I would like to return with you. I will be ready in two days. That will give me time to ask Maria. I'm sure she will have a passel of things to bring.

Alvin said, "The cabin we have for you is not furnished. It doesn't even have a stove, but we built it and the walls are sturdy and insulated with straw and the inside walls are covered, so it can be heated and stay warm. You will need all the household furniture. We will buy you a flat top wood stove so you can cook on that. We will furnish you with the staples you need, as we are bringing back enough to last the winter.

They bought another wagon and Jake along with Maria filled it with household furniture and her other trappings. Both wagons were filled to capacity. They bought two mules and were now ready to go.

Maria was in her early thirties. Her husband had died and she took a job as a cook for her livelihood. She was sweet on Jake and hung onto him when he was driving. Both Alvin and Acula liked her.

They arrived four days later and Maria was thrilled with the cabin. She knew exactly where to put everything. Jake had brought stovepipes for their stove and cut a hole in the roof and connected the stovepipe through the roof. He then caulked around it so no air or moisture could penetrate the roof.

While the women were working, Alvin showed Jake where they had been panning. He had his pan with him and picked up some sand and gravel from the edge of the creek and swirled it around and quickly saw color. He became excited, but then Alvin told him to follow him and they went to the extreme east end of where the creek went around the bulge. Alvin pointed out the seam of milky quartz that was spider webbed with gold. Jake whistled and said, "There's a fortune just where we are looking. My gosh, man, you have a bonanza, why would you share it with me?"

"Because there is enough for both of us and you know how to get to it and I don't. We are partners and may become rich."

Jake said, "That seam is on about a five degree rise toward the west. Let's walk back and see if it continues. It could come out of the ground at the west end."

"I thought of that, Jake. It doesn't. It may go back down or quit, but it doesn't show on the west end."

"I would like to go up that slope about a hundred to two hundred feet and sink a shaft. I bet we could daylight enough of that strata to make a fortune."

"Most of the bulge you see is flat on top. We have a cabin up there and a garden. However, it goes another three or more hundred feet before it slopes down to the creek. The denseness of the fir trees would keep anyone from seeing what we are doing. I know it will take blasting powder to blast out that seam of quartz. What do you think it might do to the overhang of that cliff?"

"That is something to think about. We may try to blast some of it and see what happens."

"Yes, but we better be a long ways off if we do."

"Well, no matter Alvin, I have a lot of panning to do before we get into that. I just was thinking that this winter when the creek is froze, we may want to look into it."

Jake then bent down and began panning again. He was ecstatic with what was showing in his pan. Alvin could see he knew just what he was doing and that Acula and he had just got what was on the very top.

Alvin went back to where the girls were. They were sitting drinking coffee. Maria got up and made a cup for Alvin. She then said, "This is what I've always wanted. Away from the hustle and bustle of people and alone with a man I love. Do you suppose Jake loves me?"

Alvin laughed and said, "Do you suppose he would bring you all the way out here if he didn't. If he doesn't love you, he will by the time winter is over."

It was now getting dark and Jake showed up with a large grin on his face. He said, "Alvin, you have the greatest claim I have ever worked."

These words hit Alvin's ears like a hammer, as he thought, *"I have never claimed this place. I think I will carefully sketch out this place and return to town and stake my claim.*

Two days later he came to Jake and said, "Acula and I are going back to Denver for more supplies. Do Maria and you need anything?"

Maria had a list for them and they left for Denver. Alvin had explained why they were going to Acula when he was making the sketch. Alvin made the sketch as near to scale as he could. He then triangulated the peaks that were in the area to pinpoint the bulge.

They reached Denver and asked where the land office was located. He was told, and they went directly there. The clerk had a smile on his face and said, "I'm Arthur Powell, how may I help you?"

Alvin said, "My wife and I would like to stake a claim," and handed Powell the sketch he had made. The sketch showed the length of the bulge and from a hundred feet south of the far bank of the creek to three hundred feet from the north side of the cliff. This included the entire cliff and over two hundred feet on top.

Powell saw the three peaks that Alvin had shown and brought a topographical map over that covered the area. It just took Alvin a minute or two to find the peaks. He showed them to Powell who used a ruler to triangulate the spot of the bulge. The creek was shown so it was easy to locate the claim. Powell then made a sketch of the claim on his map.

He then said, "When you return, go to each end of where the creek returns to the cliff and drill into the cliff face with a star drill deep enough to hold a paper making your claim. Then close the hole so moisture cannot damage the claim paper. Mark the spot so that it would be easy for you to find. That should do it for you. The cost is two dollars."

Alvin left the land office feeling much better about his claim. Without it, they didn't even have a claim to their cabin. They then went by the general store and loaded their wagon with the goods they needed. Alvin bought a star drill and a two pound single jack. He also bought three cases of dynamite.

While traveling back it turned very cold. They were both glad to reach home. They went directly to the corral and turned out the horses. Maria was glad to see them and helped unload the supplies.

Alvin said, "Where is Jake?"

"He's with the love of his life, that creek yonder. I swear he is there from dawn to dark. He's as happy as if he were on his honeymoon."

Acula said, "He's making you rich, Maria."

She laughed and said, "You know, I don't think he cares so much about the money. It's the finding the gold that makes him happy. I swear if you told him he had only two more days to live, he would spend it panning," and they all laughed.

Maria said, "Why don't you stay for dinner. I'm starting a stew and it's enough for all four of us. I should say six of us, as Jake eats enough for three men as he skips lunch. I tried to make him a lunch he could carry along, but he said that he doesn't want to spend the time. You ought to see how much gold he's panned," and she pulled back a clothe that covered a bucket that was half full of gold.

"My," Alvin said, "We are all getting rich."

Maria said, "Like I say, Jake doesn't care about getting rich as long as he can find the gold."

It was getting dark and Jake arrived with a large grin on his face. He said, "I've never been this happy in my live. I can pan gold all day and come back to the best cooking in the world and sleep with a beautiful woman."

"Heaven on earth," Maria sighed.

The stew was delicious and they all ate too much. Jake didn't eat near what Maria said, as he couldn't stop talking about the gold he found."

Alvin said, "Maria told us that it's not the money you are making, but the finding the gold that makes you happy."

Jake sat back and thought about that a minute. He then said, "You know she's right. It's the finding, that makes me happy. It also gives me a warm feeling to know that Maria will have security the rest of her life. I think we will get married the next time we go to Denver."

Maria laughed and said, "That will only be when the gold runs out. I might be old and gray by then."

Jake said, "Well, maybe Alvin will bring a preacher out here sometimes, and he can marry us while I pan," and they all laughed.

When the creek froze that winter Jake and Maria were up to the cabin where Acula was feeding them dinner. Jake said, "How about you and I sinking a shaft near the end of the flat place on the east end?"

Alvin said, "Why not. I don't want to get fat sitting around the cabin. We can start tomorrow hewing some of the timber there. We may need the timber for shoring. They played a game of cards that Jake showed them. It was getting late and Maria and Jake left.

Acula said, "We had better go to bed now, because Jake will be here before day break. I'll cook you both a good breakfast and have a hot meal for lunch."

The next day Jake found a place that he wanted to sink a shaft. They cut trees most of the day and removed their stumps. It was a place about ten by ten feet. It took all day to do that chore. Jake left an hour before sundown. Before he left, Jake said, "I don't like Maria down there alone. Tomorrow, I'll bring her up here. The girls will have a good time together."

Alvin said, "Tell Maria that Acula will cook breakfast."

The digging of the shaft was in soft dirt and they were able to dig several feet down along ten feet of the cliff. They also dug out five feet from the cliff. Alvin had built two ladders and put several timbers in the ditch as they got deeper.

The third day they had dug beneath the quartz strata and it had as much gold in it as the one they saw in the creek. They used the star drill and put holes for dynamite where Jake wanted them. By the sixth day, they were ready to blast. Alvin wouldn't let the women stay in the cabin. Jake set the fuses for about ten minutes. They would then have time to be across the creek and go into trees.

The blast went off and they felt the ground shake, but nothing fell from the cliff. They went to Maria's cabin and had coffee before they went back to work. Jake and Alvin spent the rest of the day removing the ore they had blasted out. They could see that strata went into the cliff although they had blasted out three feet of it and ten feet along the seam. They spent the next two days hauling the ore to another flat spot near the cabin.

Jake said, "We need to clear a working area. We should use that tarp you use for the haystack and break the ore down on that so we don't lose any of the gold."

They spent a week breaking down the gold. Maria and Acula could pick a lot of it out, but Jake panned the remainder. They were getting much more gold that Jake had done panning.

Jake said, "If we had a ball mill we could do in minutes what we do with the sledge hammer in a day."

"Could we bring a ball mill up here," Alvin asked.

Jake said, "I guess we could, but it would take mowing down a path through the trees and we don't want that. It would also require several men to assemble it. No, the ball mill is out. The word would go all over Colorado and there would be five thousand people up here in a week."

Alvin laughed and said, "I guess we will have to depend on yours and my back."

Jake said, "We're doing just fine like we are. It's hard work, but I love every minute of it."

Alvin thought, "*You might, but I would rather watch someone else work.*"

They worked all winter and now had an open pit that ran to the garden area of the cabin. They had over a hundred pounds of gold. Jake got a real kick out of melting the gold and putting it in the molds Alvin made. The seam had turn down but was still at a flat angle.

It was becoming spring and the snow had melted and the weather was warmer. Alvin said, "That hard work we did in the winter won't be as fun in the summer."

Jake said, "I'm going back to panning then."

Acula said, "Why don't we all go into Denver for a week or so and enjoy ourselves."

Maria said, "You could then marry me, Jake, or have you changed your mind."

Jake said, "No, I haven't changed my mind. I want to do that."

The four planned the trip. They carried all their gold with them. They took both wagons as they didn't want to leave any of the horses and mules behind. They left enough water and food for the goats and chickens and left.

They went to the mint to sell their gold. The Clerk said, "I'm glad you have that much gold as we were about to send for some, and it would have cost us much more. Your gold is nearly pure and easy to handle. You have just about what we need."

As they left the mint, Alvin said to Jake, "We have a bank account with the bank of Denver. You may want to deposit your money there."

Jake said, "No, I don't trust banks. I'll just keep my cash. I want to buy Maria a house. Her mother needs a place, and she can keep it up for us."

Alvin said, "We'll see you at your cabin in two days."

With that, Alvin and Acula left for the bank. At the bank they met with the vice president to discuss investments. His name was Bill Carney. Carney said, "Please don't say anything about what I want to talk to you about, as the bank likes you to invest with them. However, I have a brother named, Gene, who is the manager of the Grand Hotel.

The owner died about two weeks ago and his widow wants to sell it and move back East. My brother, Gene, says it is priced way under what it should sell for. The war has strapped everyone, so there has been no buyers. From what Gene tells me, it is the investment of a lifetime. I wish you would go talk to him. Here's the address of the hotel. He should be there now. Let me write you a note introducing you."

Alvin said, "Well, talk doesn't cost anything, so we would like to hear him out."

Acula noticed Alvin never said "I," but always "we." She thought, *"God gave me the best man on this earth,"* and said a silent prayer thanking God for giving her Alvin.

They reached the Grand and met Mr. Gene Carney. He explained that the hotel was a gold mine and that if they would buy it, he would be their partner and run it.

Gene said, "I believe I can buy the hotel for about twenty-two thousand. It cost over thirty to build and the furnishings are worth ten thousand. You will have all your investment back in three to four years. I'm telling you, this is a deal of a lifetime."

Alvin thought he was right and after discussing it with Acula, they agreed to buy it. Gene hired a lawyer to draw up the papers for a partnership, then approached the widow and offered her twenty thousand, thinking she would want twenty-five, and then they would settle on twenty-two. However, she snapped up the twenty thousand. They were now half owner in the best hotel in Denver and wouldn't have to do a thing as Gene would do all the work.

Gene said, "Being you took a chance on me, I will give you a room that I will never rent. You can keep your clothes and trappings there, so you won't have to lug them back and forth when you are in town."

They met Jake and Maria at Jakes cabin. Maria was sporting a wedding ring. Jake said, "We were married and her mother is happy in her new house. However, Maria has two brothers who are out of work. I think we should hire them. Our production would double and we could pay them three dollars a day. That is over three times what they could get here even if they could find jobs. They both have families. What do you say, Alvin?"

"We'll discuss it tonight, and let you know tomorrow. Do you think they can keep their mouths shut?"

"For three dollars a day they would have their mouths sewed up."

That night Acula said, "I think we should hire them. We will need to build them houses."

"If we are going to do that, I think we should buy a large saw and a steam engine to could run it. I would much rather tell the two men what to do than break my back every day. Jake loves the work, but I don't. I do enjoy the pleasure it gives Jake. He is happier working than making love to Maria."

Acula said, "I know it."

When they met with Jake and Maria again Alvin said, "We agree, if we can help out Maria's brothers and their families, I think we should. I want to buy a saw and a steam engine to run it. It will make it much easier to build the houses."

Jake said, "I would like to hire a carpenter. The time we lose in building the houses rather than mining will cost us a lot of money. I know a carpenter who has a teenage son. I think they could build the houses. The brother's wives could also help."

"You're right, Jake. I think we'll buy two more wagons and fill them up with the furniture they will need. We can also contract a freighting firm to bring out our supplies. Once they know the way, we can leave a standing order for the things we will need and save us a lot of time hauling things out here. As you said, every minute we spend away from the mine is costing us money."

The plan was put into place and two weeks later the houses were being built and the mine was going great guns. Maria's two brothers were Raul and Paco. Maria told them to tell everyone they were digging coal and every time they left the mine they would take coal that Acula gave them and spread it on themselves.

Everyone loved the children and they spent a lot of time fishing. Alvin took his goats down near the two houses and the carpenter made them a shed. They let the goat run free and there were now ten of them. Acula brought down some chickens and the flock grew until everyone had a nice flock of their own.

Alvin and Maria were getting water one night and looking at the houses across the river. Acula said, "We started a city. I bet one of these days there will be streets and a church."

Alvin said, "I wouldn't be surprised.

With Raul and Paco we're producing much more gold.

One day Raul's wife asked Maria, "What are they doing with all that coal?"

They are storing it for winter. They have a nice place for it. They also are hoping to find some silver, but I think that is wishful thinking."

The wagons from Denver came regularly every three months accept in the winter.

Everyone seemed to be happy. The kids came up to Acula's and Alvin's cabin everyday for school. Acula taught them to read and write. The wives of Paco and Raul came also as neither could speak English.

Acula loved to teach and Maria did the cooking for all. The carpenter and his son stayed on, as they had now built at cook house that had a dinning hall with it. They served two meals a day. Acula fed lunch to the workers and the families.

By the next spring they had over two hundred pounds of gold and had accumulated a mountain of dirt and float. They decided to take the spring off and go back to Denver. Only Jake and Maria wanted to stay. They said they would go when Maria's brothers and their families came back.

Alvin caught Jake alone and said, "Acula and I want to take some time off. We want to travel some. Acula has never seen an ocean and I would love to take her to Chicago and New York. Will you mind me going?"

"No, I think you should take some time off. We may do the same thing when you return."

When they left, they took the two hundred pounds of gold. The mint took it even though they could not use it all. The over run was sent to the Philadelphia mint. They deposited half in Jakes account and half in their account.

At their hotel, Gene Carney told them they were making much more than he thought. He sent Alvin and Acula's half of the profits to their bank's savings account. They were more than wealthy, now.

CHAPTER 6

A NEW ADVENTURE

They were in their hotel room and were sitting in two overstuffed chairs sipping some cider. Acula said, "We are still relatively young. With all the people around us, I feel crowded. Have you ever wanted to just strikeout to see if we could make it across the mountains by ourselves?"

Alvin said, "You mean leave all of this behind and just strikeout over the mountains like a pair of pioneers?"

"Yes, I would like to see some new country before the white men takes it all. Country that no white man has ever seen or been in. There's a whole world out there that I want to see. I guess really, I just want us to be alone again, with no one around us, but mother nature."

"What about the Indians? There are still the Ute, and they don't like strangers."

"I'm a Ute, and you speak Ute. We could dress like they do and they would accept us. Look at Kit Carson. He travels the Ute country with no problem."

"I'm surely no Kit Carson. They know and respect him because of his abilities. He can also charm an Indian. I surely can't."

"You surely charmed me."

"Yes, but you needed me, and it took some time. They surely don't need me and we will have no time to get them to like us."

"I'll do the talking for us, as I will tell them you are touched in the head."

"If we decide to go, you won't be lying," and Acula laughed.

Alvin said, "If that is what you really want, then let's do it."

They bought items that they would need for a long journey. They decided to go on foot and just carry backpacks. They would leave in early spring and make their way over the Rocky Mountains and see what the other side looked like. They would then decide where else they wanted to see.

They explained what they were about to do to Jake and Maria. Jake said, "Are you touched in the head? Why wouldn't you go to Chicago or New York City and live the good life?"

Acula said, "To us, this is a better way of life. We can live with mother nature."

Jake just shook his head.

Alvin said, "If we aren't back in five years, just assume we are dead and have a good time with the money. Jake, you and Maria move up to our cabin. You are in charge now and I will give you a piece of paper that will give you complete authority." Actually Alvin had already had a lawyer draw up the paper before they left Denver.

They left in early April. There were still patches of snow on the upper slopes. They were both dressed in buckskin and took the essentials for traveling. They had let their hair grow. Acula braided her hair like most squaws did, and Alvin let his hair grow also, although he did shave.

They decided to go straight over the mountains. They weren't in a hurry. Both had good rifles and handguns. They didn't go far in one day as their path took them straight up. It was very cold above ten thousand feet, and the air was thin. They found a rock overhang and made camp. They could still see the lights from the small village they had started.

Acula made a fire as Alvin gathered firewood. She had a pot of water going when Alvin returned. He had shot a rabbit and Acula gutted it and cut it up to be in a stew. Very little conversation went on as the worked.

Acula said, "The air here is like drinking cold water it is so fresh. I feel like chains have been taken away from my body, and I am free."

Alvin said, "I like it too, Acula. I am here in the wilds with you. I see what you mean. We are freer."

Alvin banked the fire and they got ready for bed. As they laid looking at a spectacular sky, Acula said, "I wish we could go to those stars. I wonder if they are worlds like ours?"

Alvin said, "I have no idea. Someday they may figure out how to get there." They then fell silent and were soon asleep.

The next day, they were off again. They went at a slow pace observing everything. They made little noise traveling. Both enjoyed the hike and at around ten in the morning, they stopped and had some coffee. They were next to a small stream that had a pool where the rocks had made a natural dam.

Alvin had taken some fishing line and some hooks. They could see some trout and he put on a little goat cheese on the hook and threw it into the water. He was rewarded instantly with a strike. He pulled in a trout, unhooked him and threw his line back out. Again, a trout took his bait. Acula gutted them and started a fire. Alvin had built a skewer for the fish and put them over the fire. Ever so often he would turn them while Acula gathered some wild kale and onions. They packed away the fish, kale and onions and traveled on.

Their stop for lunch was brief as they had their food and with a small fire that heated the fish Alvin had caught, she filled them with kale and onions that gave the fish a better taste. They were not in a hurry and stopped often to observe the landscape.

It took a week to reach the summit of the first mountain. They could see both sides of the mountains. However it was so cold that they didn't stay long and moved on down to a campsite among some boulders. There were no trees as they were still above the timberline.

The next day they didn't stop until they reached the tree line. Alvin set his trap along a small game trail hoping to trap a small animal. He used some of the kale that Acula had gathered to bait it. They were in their blankets early that night.

The next morning Alvin could see smoke a great distance off. He pointed it out to Acula and she said, "That will be a Ute village. I would like to go there and live among them awhile. Maybe my brothers are with them. We both have deep tans and they will think me one of them."

It began to rain, and they put on their slickers and traveled on. They didn't get there until dusk, and by that time the rain had stopped. They walked into the village and Acula asked a squaw where the chief's tent was. The squaw took her. They both noticed that very few of the Ute were up and about.

After reaching the tent of the chief, the squaw entered and shortly the chief appeared. He invited them into a warm fire. Two women laid on mats, with one woman tending them.

Acula explained that she was a Ute from another village and that the man with her was her husband. The chief asked them to sit by the fire. Nothing was said for awhile, then the chief told of sickness that had passed through the tribe and had killed over half of them. The sickness was now ebbing, but the entire village was hurting. It seemed to effect the men and children worse than the women. Nearly all the children were dead and three quarters of the men. Some men were recovering, but were very weak. Only a few braves were left to feed the rest. They had no horses as they had been raided just a few weeks ago by the Kiowa, but they had taken only the horses when they saw that the village was wracked with sickness.

Acula expressed that they would like to help. The chief was grateful and told them that there were plenty of empty tepees. The squaw that had shown them to the chief had remained with them, and showed them to an empty tepee next to the chief. The tepee must have belonged to an elder, because it had many features including a floor made of buffalo hides.

The next day they looked in on the sick. They found two white men. The were both very sick. One said in a weak voice that the tribe took them in because they could not stay in their saddles. Alvin tended to them. Acula was afraid that Alvin would be infected, but he said, "Whether I get sick or not, I must help."

The first thing that Alvin told the chief was that the disease may be caused by the water they drank, and advised all water they drank or cooked with to be boiled. The chief immediately told the tribe that the sickness came from the water and had to be boiled before drinking. After that, no one else became sick.

The two white men were trappers. They had lost their horses, also, when the Kiowa raided. Alvin then began to think how they could get the horses back.

The chief knew they had to wait until all the men were healthy, then they may be able to steal the horses back from the Kiowa.

Three weeks passed and the white trappers were healthy again. The tribe then began to plan how they would get their horses back. They sent out scouts and located the Kiowa and then made there plan. They would get within a couple of miles of them, then go in. The scouts told them the horses were kept in a brush corral. The plan was to start in late afternoon. They would have two braves get inside the corral and light the brush afire and drive the horses out. The two white trappers, Alvin and Acula would line up with their repeating rifles, and fire their weapons as fast as they could to discourage the Kiowa from pursuing them. They would then fall back and four braves would form a line and shoot as they had. Then all of them would retreat.

The plan was solid. The only flaw was that the two Ute scouts had been seen, so the Kiowa were aware that there would be a raid.

When they were within two miles of the Kiowa camp. They camped. Just before they started on the raid, Alvin had to make a call of nature. He went into a thick stand of pines that was near a bluff. He noticed a deadfall had fell against the bluff where a ledge protruded. The limbs of the deadfall were such that Alvin could climb up to the ledge, which he did. The ledge had an indenture that was almost a cave. He looked in and could see many bones. Alvin knew it was the den of a mountain lion, but it had not been used lately as he noticed spider webs were about.

He made note of this, as Acula had always told him to look for places to hide incase of an emergency. Alvin didn't think he would ever need this hiding place, but he thought it a good place if he had to hole up for awhile.

CHAPTER 7

WAR AND RUNNING

They were off to their raid. It went down just like they thought it would. The brush was lit and the horses driven. However, as the trappers, Alvin and Acula lined up to fire, a hail of bullets came at them. The first hit was Alvin. A bullet creased his skull and he went down. The rest fired, but the hail of bullets took them.

When Acula fell beside Alvin, he could tell she was dead as a bullet had penetrated her skull. He had no time to mourn, as he knew he must move or die.

The wind was up and a thunder cloud burst sending hail the size of plums down so thickly that it was hard to stand. Alvin quickly took Acula's pack and put her rifle through the straps. He put that pack over his head. The back of the backpack rested on his backpack as he ran. He held on to the rifle which was threaded through the two straps. This sheltered him from the intense hail.

He ran back as fast as he could. It was hard to see as the hail was coming down so thickly. The hail now turned into a torrential downpour that nearly blinded him. However, he walked on as quickly as he could. The rain began to lessen when he was about a quarter of a mile away. He could see some of the Ute on the ground that were dead. With the downpour Alvin could barely make his way.

An hour later he got his bearings as light began to appear in the west. He began thinking of the den on that ledge. He knew the Kiowa would not rest until they killed them all. By dusk, he found the deadfall and climbed up to the ledge. He went in the den and sat down. He decided to sleep if he could, so he took his and Acula's bedrolls and tried to sleep. He was so exhausted that he slept, but fitfully.

When he awoke, he immediately thought of Acula. What a wonderful woman she had been. He knew he must not dwell on his sadness, as he had plenty to do to survive. He thought of building a fire, but then thought of the smoke and smell. He smiled as he thought of all the things Acula had taught him. Had she not, he would have no chance of survival.

As he had a good place for now, he knew his best bet was to stay put. He looked around at his surroundings. He saw that a large crack ran through the cave and vertically up and down the bluff. It was nearly a foot wide. He wondered if he started a fire, would the smoke go up into that crack. He really wanted a cup of coffee. He decided to chance it. He broke a lot of branches off the dead fall. The packrats had made nests that would give him the necessary fodder to start a fire. He got everything ready and was just about to light his fire, when he heard voices. He could tell it was the Kiowa looking for the Ute.

Alvin got his two rifles ready and waited. The voices sounded like they were going away. An hour later he heard nothing. He then lit his fire and boiled some coffee and ate some bread that Acula had put in her backpack. He waited another day before he decided to leave. He had decided to go a different direction from either of the tribes. The Kiowa were to the north and the Ute were to the south. He decided to go west as Acula had wanted to go. He thought he would go to the Pacific Ocean because Acula wanted to see it.

He was still in mountainous terrain, so the going was slow. He camped that night by a small pool of water that a small stream cascaded into. He used his fishing line and caught a couple of small trout. He enjoyed them thinking of Acula.

After a week, the mountains turned into barren canyons. He turned due north, now. He had both Acula's and his canteens, but he knew his biggest trial of survival would be finding water. Acula had talked about this to him. She had told him that animals and insects needed water just like humans and to follow their tracks. They would lead him to water. This proved true, but the waterholes were very far apart and the animal tracks few.

Although he knew his problem, he didn't hurry. He took his time and rationed his water the best he could. He went two days dry and thought he may not make it, but then the terrain started changing and he came to a river. He had heard of the White River, and thought this may be it. He crossed the river at a rocky part that was shallow and went west along it for a mile or two until he saw a good place to camp. He had noticed antelope tracks and decided to see where they watered. He found a good place to wait, and that evening he killed a doe. He spent the next day stripping the meat and smoking it. He had found many wild onions and other plants that Acula had shown him.

His thoughts most of the day were about Acula and the many things she taught him. He thought how at first he had no love for her, but as time went on, her kindness turned to like, and then to love. The way she would look at him with such adoring eyes. Yes, it was the way she looked at him, that made him begin to love her, then adore her.

He left the river well provisioned and went north. He found an old trail that was going north. He knew the transcontinental railroad had been completed and that it ran through southern Wyoming. He decided to go mostly north to intercept the railroad. He wasn't in any hurry, and decided to enjoy the trip as he knew that Acula would have. Many things reminded him of her. He tried to take her from his mind, but it was no use. Everything in nature reminded him of her.

He had traveled three more days, then spotted some smoke. It was a lot of smoke. He then began to see buildings. He thought it might just be a ranch, but it was more than that. As he got closer he could tell it was a town. He could see a smoke stack that was making the smoke. It looked like a smelter, but smaller than smelters he had seen before. He knew it was a mining operation, as he could see a ball mill. It was higher than the town and was on a shelf that ran up to a bluff. He could see a house away from the mining operation. It was a large house. One like he had seen pictures of on the old southern plantations. There were several other structures behind the main house.

There was a village below all this. There were many houses in the village on laid out streets. He had eaten all his jerky and had missed the last two meals. He decided to approach a log cabin that sat on the edge of town. It sat within a cull-de-sac, with hills on both sides. In front of the cabin, maybe fifty feet, was a spring that steam came from and sometimes spurted in the air a few feet. The cabin was above the spring and backed into the cull-de-sac. He walked around the spring and knocked on the cabin door. A woman of over forty opened the door. She wore a robe and her hair was messed like she had been in bed.

Alvin said, "I'm Alvin Scott and I have been traveling for several weeks. I have run out of food and wondered if you would be kind enough to feed me."

The woman said, "I'm ill, but you are welcome to come in and fix yourself a meal. I must get back in bed as I am very weak."

"Is there anything I can do to help you, Madam?"

"No, my daughter is at work and she tends to me. I hate to prevail upon you, but we need firewood to cook. The house is naturally heated by the warm ground. Just put your hand on the slate floor."

Alvin bent down and felt the slate, it was very warm. He noticed that the cabin was warm and there was no fire in the fireplace. He said, "I would be glad to gather firewood, and do any other chores you may need."

The woman smiled and said, "I see you are a good man. Since my husband left, we have been hard put to survive. I hope you will stay with us awhile until I am on my feet again or my husband returns."

"Where did your husband go?"

"He spoke out against Martin Brunel. He was summoned to Mr. Brunel's house and has not returned. That was five weeks ago. My daughter obtained a job at the general store as a clerk. She makes fifty cents a day, six days a week. That gives us three dollars. It is barely enough to buy the few groceries that we need. My husband worked in the mine that is owned by Mr. Brunel, so even if Lon returns, he will probably be out of a job."

"What do you suppose happened to him?"

"My daughter asked several people, but none of them knew or didn't want to say. I think Mr. Brunel had him killed. Lon was a fine carpenter. He drank too much and when he did he spouted off. That is something no one does, if they want to stay healthy. Mr. Brunel runs everything around here with an iron fist. He doesn't have a son anymore. He was killed in the war. Since then, Brunel has become bitter and vicious. I understand he pays his men well, as that is the only way he could keep them.

"Holley, my daughter, is such a sweet girl. She does everything around here, now that I'm laid up."

"What is your illness, if I'm not getting too personal?"

"It's like the flu, but has lingered. It came on about the time Lon left."

Alvin went out and found an axe in a tool shed. The tool shed was large and must have doubled as a place to keep a horse as there was a stall there and a small amount of hay. He noted the precision with which the tool house and the cabin were made. It was the work of a skilled carpenter.

Alvin cut up nearly a cord of wood before he came back into the house. He then brought in an arm load of wood and left the rest near the door. He built a fire and then made himself some pancakes. There was no syrup, but Alvin was so hungry he didn't miss it.

He said, "May I fix you some broth, Mrs......" She finished by saying, "Alton, Elizabeth Alton. No, we have nothing to use for broth. Holley will bring something for that tonight. She will be peeved at me for letting you in, but I could tell you were a gentleman and we do need a man around here."

Holley was surprised to see Alvin. She had first noticed the firewood stacked near the door and was glad that chore was done. When she opened the door, Alvin arose. She was shocked and looked at her mother.

Elizabeth said, "Holley, this is Mr. Scott. He has come to help us through our hard times. He has already cut wood and fixed that sagging door."

Holley addressed Alvin in not so friendly a manner. She asked, "Where did you come from. Brunel didn't send you did he?"

"No Miss Alton. I have been traveling for several weeks. My wife and I were ambushed by Indians. They killed her and I miraculously escaped with my life. Others with us were all killed. I ran out of food yesterday and prevailed on your poor mother for food. I can pay you and will. However, with the trouble that has transpired, I think I had better keep away from town and will give you the money." He took a ten dollar gold piece from his pocket and extended his hand towards Holley.

She did not take it. She said, "I'm not sure I want you to stay with us. I know nothing about you, other than you say you have been traveling for weeks. I see you are armed, unshaven and dirty, other than that, I don't know anything about you."

"That is the way for anyone who one meets. I can clean up by your spring. If you will take my money, you can buy many items that you need. I see most of your staples are gone. I will keep out of your way and do anything you require. I just need to stay a couple of days. I want to rest up and then proceed north to intercept the railroad."

Elizabeth said, "I have talked to him and he is a fine man."

"Why were you and your wife in Indian country?" Holly asked.

"My wife is part Indian and she wanted to look for her family. She gave up a trip to Europe, to go and see them. We found some of her people, but the men were all stricken with sickness. Before we arrived the Kiowa came and took all their horses. They wanted the women, but saw that many were sick, so they took none of them.

"The tribe wanted their horses back and planned a raid on the Kiowa to get them back. They wanted both myself and my wife to come as we had repeating rifles and were both good shots. The raid went awry, and they were waiting for us. A bullet creased my skull and knocked me down," Alvin turned his head to show the crease, "It knocked me down. That is all that saved my life, for a hail of bullets came that killed everyone in our group. A hail storm then came and I was able to slip away. They hunted me and others for a few days, but I found a hiding place and had enough provisions to stay in one place. I then slipped away and for weeks went north, as I want to catch the train and go back to Denver."

"What do you do in Denver?"

"We or now I, am half owner of the Grand Hotel. I also am part owner of a mine west of Denver."

"My, you seem well heeled."

"I am and I can get you and your mother on your feet again if you'll let me."

"I hope you don't think that will buy you extra favors."

"No, I am recently widowed and loved my wife dearly."

"Well, you can use that loft," and she pointed to a loft on the north wall. I will show you a place down by the spring that we use as a bathtub. Dad, built a shelter around it. I think there is still soap and a towel there for you."

Alvin again extended his arm with the ten dollar gold piece and she took it.

She said, "I'm going back to the store. Do you have something smaller that that gold piece, they may wonder where I got it."

"Yes, I believe I have five one dollar notes." He took out his wallet and thumbed through a wad of large bills. Holley was awed at the amount of money Alvin carried.

Alvin found four, one dollar bills and said, "Please don't tell anyone that I have money. This Brunel may pounce on me. Please, also, inquire about a horse. When I leave here, I will want to be mounted."

"I won't ask about the horse, we are already being looked at by Brunel's people. He has spies everywhere. He stopped the stage from coming to High Grove, because he didn't want people coming and going. He uses the road for shipping his gold and didn't want people on the road. He owns the livery stable, so I wouldn't go there."

"Is there anyone who owns horses, besides Brunel?"

"Yes, Ernest Gray has a farm on the other side of town. You may be able to get a horse from him, but I understand he's a skinflint and will want a high price if he realizes you're in a bind."

"Are there any nice people in High Grove?"

"A few, I suppose. Mr. Elder who owns the general store is nice, but his wife isn't. She was mad at him for hiring me. He told her that he couldn't get anyone to work for fifty cents a day, so she let off of him, but makes sure he's not around me when she's not there. My gosh, the man is over fifty."

"Well, you are a handsome woman and all men like young handsome women."

"Even you?" Holley smiled.

"Even me."

After Alvin left for his bath, Elizabeth said, "He's a handsome man, Holley. You may not see another nice, young man in this town."

"You're right, there, mother. However, he is grieving for his wife, so I have little chance there."

"There is always a chance. Try to get him to stay on for awhile. Blame it on me. Tell him you don't want for me to be alone all day, and to tell the truth, I like him."

When Alvin reached the bathhouse, the water was warm to hot. It was nice. He also washed all his clothes. He had kept a clean shirt, trousers and underwear, so he had a complete change. He was gone nearly an hour. When He came back he had shaved and cut his hair as best he could, and he looked completely different. He was a handsome man."

When he entered the cabin, Holley gasped.

"It's me," Alvin said. "I took off some of the bark."

"You look much nicer. I hope you will stay around for awhile until mother gets better."

"I need to see about a horse. I will skirt town tomorrow and come in from the west. I'll tell Gray my horse broke its leg and I had to shoot him. I will then bargain for a horse. If he tries to hold me up, I'll just tell him Brunel will sell me one much cheaper. Then, I think I'll get a better price."

CHAPTER 8

ADJUSTING TO A NEW HOME

The next day, Alvin went to Gray's farm. Gray could tell he was sharp, and gave him a good price on a gilding. Alvin asked that Gray keep the animal for awhile. As Gray could see he could use his horse, he agreed.

After getting papers on the horse, Alvin then walked into town. He saw a feed store and asked the owner to deliver a bale of hay and a sack of corn to the Alton cabin. He said, it was a debt he owed them.

Alvin took note of the town. There was a blacksmith shop, a hotel, a gambling parlor with upstairs rooms for sporting women. There was a tavern, a clothing store, the general store, where Holley worked, a feed store and several other businesses on the main street, which was actually the only street with businesses. A church and a school sat near the end of the street. It was mid-afternoon and no one was in the saloon.

Alvin ordered a beer and then asked. Does Brunel own this saloon?"

"No, however, he owns nearly everything else. Other than the mine, he owns the hotel and the livery stable. If he asked to buy me out, I would have to sell, as he would not permit people to come in here."

"How can he do that?"

"He owns the mine the smelter and the ball mill, that employ most of the men in this town."

Alvin nodded then said, "I had a friend in Virginia City who asked me to look up a friend of his, if I were ever through High Grove. Let's see his name was Alfred, no Olton, no…."

"Alton," the barkeep said.

"Yes, that was it, do you know him?"

"Yes, but that's is all I will say."

"How's that?"

"It's not healthy to even mention his name."

"I don't understand, what could be unhealthy about just knowing someone?"

"I will say this only once. Never mention Alton's name. Brunel may have you killed for just saying the name."

"He has that much power?"

"He owns the law, the judge and most of the people who would sit at your trial."

"Why do you stay here, I would move out tomorrow."

"Everything I have, is tied up in this saloon. Unless someone offers to buy it, I'm stuck."

"Well, you have one friend in this town, and that's me."

"Why did you come here?"

"I'm just passing through. I guess I will pay my respects to the Alton family and move on. Where do they live?"

"In a cabin, just east of town. If I were you, I would just go on, the Alton name is not too popular with Brunel."

"Well, he may own you, but he doesn't own me."

"If he decides to come after you, you'll be sorry. He has five men who are around him most of the time. He decides who comes and who goes. He stopped the stage from coming here, and he wouldn't let the telegraph come here either."

"Well, he can't stop the post office. He's not bigger than the federal government."

"No, but he controls the people who work for the post office, so he might as well own that, too."

"Is there a print shop in town?"

"There use to be. There was also a newspaper, but somehow the owner left and no one has seen him since. He left everything he owned behind."

"You mean Brunel killed him?"

"I didn't say that. I just know that one day he was here, and the next day he wasn't. He had just printed a scathing article about Brunel."

Alvin had an idea. He smiled and the barkeep said, "What's funny?"

"Nothing. I just thought of something. I've got to go. By the way, how does Mrs. Alton get by without a husband?"

"She has a daughter who works at the general store. Please don't go by there. It will just cause Holley a lot of trouble. Please leave them alone."

"I guess you're right. I guess I'll just pull out and leave well enough alone."

"Where is the nearest town north of High Grove?"

"That would be Craig or Steamboat Springs. Most of the supply wagons use the road to Steamboat Springs. They are both about fifty miles away, but there is some rugged country between there and here. Meeker is west and is closer, but there's nothing much there. I hear a railroad is coming through Craig from Steamboat Springs. It will take them awhile to build it through that country.

"Any Indian trouble between here and Craig?"

"No trouble. There's Indians, Arapahoe, but they are friendly to whites as they like to trade."

Alvin left going towards the livery stable, like he was going to get his horse. However, he just went through the backdoor and on to the Alton cabin, as no one could see him.

That night, Holley came home with an arm load of groceries. They had a good meal that night. At the table, Alvin said, "I'm going hunting tomorrow and may be gone a few days. We need fresh meat."

Before daybreak the next day Alvin woke up Gray and told him he would be taking his horses. He had bought a saddle from Gray. He paid too much, but he just marked it down to make it up on any later transaction with Gray.

Alvin was on his way before the sun came up. He traveled due north. He met an Indian a few miles out of town. The Indian knew English and Alvin asked about a trail to Craig. The Indian told him and they parted a few miles later.

He didn't get to Craig that day, but around noon the next day he rode into town. He first put his animal in the livery stable, then got a room at the local hotel. After eating lunch, he inquired about a printing shop.

At the printing shop, he told the owner he was playing a joke on someone. He wanted posters printed saying:

WANTED - MARTIN BRUNEL
$10,000 DEAD OR ALIVE

The poster didn't say who was to pay the ten-thousand.

The shop owner said, "I know Brunel, he won't sleep until he finds who posted these."

"Yes, if he is still alive. Some of his own bodyguards may do him in."

"You know this is against the law, don't you? However, I won't say anything as I know the man. I think he did away with a friend of mine in High Grove. There is nothing they can trace going back to us about the poster. So, I'm in this as much as you are. Just don't get caught or we both may be lying in a shallow grave. There is no charge."

Alvin left two hours before day break and being he knew the trail now, made it by nightfall. He camped and was up two hours before daybreak. He had purchased some thumbtacks from the printer and by four in the morning had all ten of the posters put up outside all the stores in town.

He then rode to the Alton place. There he found the bale of hay and the sack of corn. He came in the door as he saw a light burning. Holley was dressed and was just starting breakfast. She was glad to see him.

Alvin said, "I never saw a thing. However, I bought a horse. I think I will use the tool shed as a stall for it, if it is alright with you."

"Dad had a horse and he used the tool shed to house him, so go right ahead."

After breakfast Alvin went out and changed things around some, so he could get the animal into the tool shed. He then put the door back on. He built a trough to put the oats and hay in. He then started building a corral that extended down to the Spring. He would only close the tool shed when the weather was bad.

Holley came home at noon with the news. She said, "Someone posted notices all over town that Brunel was wanted dead or alive for ten thousand dollars. Do you think someone will kill him?"

"Who knows. People are really greedy."

It took Alvin three days to build the corral, so the town people was unable to know him. At supper that night, Alvin said, "You might tell people your cousin came in last night and is planning to stay awhile."

"Yes, I think that's a good idea."

"I think in a day or so I will apply for a job as a miner. I would like to get acquainted with the layout that Brunel has."

"I'm not sure that would be wise, Alvin. Brunel would be able to keep a close watch on you. I have heard that he does that with new employees."

"You may be right. I'll think on that some more. However, I would like to see more of the town and let people know me more, as suspicion can cause a lot of trouble. I will apply for odd jobs. I noticed a bakery near where you work. I don't know much about baking, but I can learn."

The baker said, "I can use you during holidays. Where are you staying?"

"I'm a nephew of Mrs. Alton and am staying there."

"Alton, oh my, he's the chap who's missing."

"Yes, Mrs. Alton needs me, now, but her chores don't keep me busy, so I thought I would try to get some odd jobs."

"You might ask Mr. Elder. He sometimes needs a driver to pick up things that the regular suppliers don't bring. Brunel lets the suppliers use the road to Steamboat Springs on days he is not delivering gold and silver."

Alvin came into the Elder's general store. He said hello to Holley and then went to see Mr. Elder. Elder said, "Yes, I can't keep a driver. They all quit when they are hoorayed by Brunel's drivers."

"Why would they pick on another driver?"

"Many of Brunel's men think they are something special because they work for Brunel."

"Where do they do their drinking?"

"At Minnie's Gambling Hall. She has sporting women that they like."

Alvin thought, *I need to get the bluff on these men early or I'll get the same treatment."*

That night he slicked down his hair with some grease. He put on a nice shirt he had bought that made him look like the kind that gun-slicks wore. He put on his scabbard and six-shooter and tied down his scabbard like he had seen others do."

Holley said, "You may get into trouble wearing a gun. Why don't you leave it at home?"

"No, I need it to prove a point. I'll tell you about it later."

He entered Minnie's about eight that evening. He kept to himself at the end of the bar nursing a rye. The man next to him was dressed like a lot of teamsters he had seen. The man said, "I haven't seen you around here before."

Alvin said, "This is the first time I've been to Minnie's. I generally do my drinking at the saloon."

"What do you do stranger?"

"I was just hired by Mr. Elder to drive a supply wagon."

"The man laughed and said, "Did you hear that Marvin? We have another teamster that drives for Elder. We don't cotton to other drivers. I suggest you quit."

"I suggest you shut your big mouth before I blow your head off." Alvin then turned to the man in a gunfighters stance.

The man was shocked and said, "Do you know who we are?"

"Yes, a loud mouthed, stinking teamster that smells like horse shit. If you and your partner want trouble, that's my middle name," and he glared at them, then said, "Well, what will it be, Loud Mouth?"

The teamster said, "We were just funning, we didn't mean anything by it. We often do that to strangers just to get a rise out of them."

"You won't do it anymore or you will be in boot hill. Now turn around and take a table, I don't want you near me when I'm drinking."

The two teamsters left the bar and went to a table. The barkeep came over and said, "Have a rye on the house stranger. I'm Lester Dale. Those two have had that coming for awhile. They'll think twice before they hoorah another person."

"I don't like trouble, but neither do I shy from it."

Another man slid down the bar to where the teamsters had been. He said, "I'm Hal Watson. I own a ranch west of town. I like the way you handle yourself. Have you done any cow punching? I'm looking for a good man."

"I've done my share, but I promised Mr. Elder I would drive his wagon and I always keep my word if I can."

"That is another trait I admire, Mr........."

"Alvin Scott. I'm new in town. I'm a nephew of Mrs. Alton, and just came to help, now that her husband has disappeared. No one seems to know anything about it. When I ask, people, they just turn away, as if they are scared of something."

"I know nothing about his disappearance. He was here one day and gone the next."

"My aunt said, he received a message from Mr. Brunel to come to his house, but never came home."

"I would drop that now, if I were you. Brunel can be viscous if someone gets into his business."

"So you think Brunel did away with my uncle?"

"I didn't say that. Let's change the subject. It isn't healthy to talk about Mr. Brunel. Your uncle did, and now he's gone." With that, Hal Watson turned away and left.

The barkeep came back over and said, "Hal Watson is a good man. Everybody is scared of Brunel. I can't blame them. You buck him, and you disappear."

"I understand there's a ten-thousand dollar reward on his head. Do you think someone will try to collect?"

"You never know. I wouldn't be surprised if someone takes a shot at him. He pays those close to him well, but there are many people who have a grudge against him."

"Well, I never cottoned to blood money, no matter who it is or how much is offered.

CHAPTER 9

A NEW IMAGE

The two teamsters were talking to their boss the next day as the wagons were being loaded. Buster said, "We ran into a guy who is working for Elder, driving his supply wagon."

"Did you give him the ole hoorah as usual?"

"No, he's a gunfighter and braced Marvin and me. We could see we wouldn't have a chance against him, so we walked away."

"I never knew you two to back down. Are you getting old and soft?"

"Go to Minnie's tonight and brace him if you're so brave."

"Me? I'm no gunfighter."

"Neither are we. Why don't you mention it to one of Brunel's bodyguards. They may want to brace him to show what big men they are."

"I don't think so. They put on a big show, but I've never seen them in action. Besides, Brunel may not like it, and we would all be in hot water."

"Yeah, you're right. Let's just drop it, before it costs us all. Brunel is really on his high horse lately. It's because Lacy walked out on him. He got her from a saloon in Craig. He never will marry anyone. He's too selfish. She just saddled up and rode out in the middle of the night. Guess she got enough of his guff. Since she left, he's gotten a lot meaner. He slapped one of the cooks yesterday, and broke off one of her teeth. He then fired her because she looked ugly with the missing tooth. She's Mexican, so no one cares one way or the other."

"She has a brother in Mexico. I hear he rides with a gang. He may come up here. Wouldn't that be something. I would like to see a big fight. Those five who are his bodyguards have never been tested. I wonder what they would do if that Mexican gang came up here."

"Yeah, that would be something."

Someone had told one of the five bodyguards about the gunfighter backing down the teamster's of Brunel. He told Brunel. Brunel said, "It may be a bounty hunter looking for that ten-thousand dollar bounty. Check it out Delbert."

"It's too early for a bounty hunter to be up here."

"I said check it out, damn it!"

"Yes Sir, Mr. Brunel."

The next night Alvin was in the saloon. There was just two other men there. Both miners. Delbert had gone down to Minnie's place, but no one had seen the gunfighter. Everyone now knew about Alvin bracing the two teamsters."

Delbert then went to the saloon and there stood Alvin talking to the barkeep. Delbert sauntered up to the bar and ordered a rye. He then turned to Alvin and said, "The whole town is talking about how you backed down those two teamsters last night."

"I wasn't asking for trouble, but they brought it to me. I hate to kill someone over such a trivial matter, but if someone pushes me, I push back."

Alvin had already noticed the way the man wore his gun. In a matter of fact manner, Alvin said, "Are you here to push the matter," and turned to face the man with his hand near his gun.

"Noooo. I was sent here by my boss to check you out. He thinks you may be a bounty hunter."

"Like I was telling the barkeep here, I don't cotton to blood money."

"I tried to tell the boss that, as it would be too early for anyone to show up. Those posters only went up yesterday. I want to thank you for putting Marvin and Buster in their place. They were beginning to think they were roosters, when in fact they're pigeons," and he laughed. Alvin did not laugh. He just stood facing the man talking, like he was ready for anything. Delbert could see he may be looking at something he didn't want.

Delbert then said, "Thank you, Sir," and walked out. As he walked out the door he thought, *That guy was ready to blow my head off. He's pure poison. I'll make sure I avoid him. I better tell Fred, Luke, Paul and Pete to ride clear of him. No use getting our heads blown off for nothing.*

Delbert went directly to Mr. Brunel and said, "I met the fellow and asked him if he had seen the wanted poster. He said he didn't cotton to blood money, and hated anyone who did." Delbert always embellished every story.

Delbert added, "I liked the man. He just backed down Marvin and Buster because they hoorayed him. It served them right, I would have done the same in his place."

"Thanks Delbert, I can always count on you and the boys. I think those posters were just put there to worry me. However, you boys be very careful, ten-thousand is a lot of money."

The other boys were standing around when Delbert made his report and after Brunel went to his room to read, the others came around him asking questions. Delbert said, "I didn't want to worry Mr. Brunel, but that man is pure poison. He could be anyone, Clay Allison, Mort Davis or any of those gunfighters. I've never seen any of them, but I know a killer when I see one. When I talked to him, he turned toward me, never taking his eyes off me. He just looked holes into my face, like he was ready for anything. I've heard that gunfighters never take chances, that's why they stay alive."

"We're suppose to be gunfighters, Delbert."

Delbert laughed and said, "That guy is meaner than fifty of us. I wish you could have seen the look. He didn't even blink as he watched me expecting that I might draw. If he knew what was going on in my brain, he would have laughed.

Fred said, "We're a mean bunch aren't we," and they all laughed.

"I would hate it if Brunel knew we were all bluff," said Pete.

"Well it worked," said Paul. "That was a stoke of genius telling Brunel you knew four other gunfighters as good as yourself, Delbert."

"Well, I didn't lie," and they all laughed.

Brunel heard them laugh from his room and came into the room and said, "What is so funny in here, Delbert?"

"We were just laughing at how tough Marvin and Buster were when they took on a pilgrim and how they took water when they met a gunfighter."

"Yeah, that was funny. However, they're good teamsters, just not too tough," and they all laughed.

***

The word about the brace of Marvin and Buster went around town like a wildfire. The barkeep at the saloon also told how Alvin looked at Delbert, and how Delbert got out of the saloon as soon as he could.

That evening at dinner, Holley said, "The word all over town is about what a mean gunfighter you are. What did you do?"

"Nothing. A couple of teamsters who work for Brunel tried to hoorah me and I turned to them with as mean a face as I could muster and said, "Do you want to back that up? They backed down and that was all there was to it. People always want to make something more than there is in a boring place. I remember the army. Now if you want a boring place, just join the army. Everything that happens is blown up twice the size, as what actually happened. It's just a way of dealing with boredom."

"Well, you certainly have a reputation now."

"Good, maybe people will not pick on me. I met one of Brunel's bodyguards last night. He was sent by Brunel to see if I were a bounty hunter. I told him I didn't cotton to blood money. He said that he told Brunel the same thing, because it was too soon for a bounty hunter to show up. I even had him sweating, because I turned and faced him and keep looking him straight in the eye not saying a word after that. He left abruptly."

"Well, Mother, don't you feel safer having Wild Bill Hickok living with us?" And they all laughed.

After supper, Alvin helped Holley with the dishes. She said, "Tell me about your wife, Alvin?"

"I would rather not. It is just too sad for me. I'll never find a woman who adored me like she did. I could just read it in her face. Losing her was worse than losing my own life. I carry on for her, as that is what she would have wanted. That's all I will say on that subject."

Holley repeated the words. "'She adored you,' what a wonderful thing to say. It would be easy to love someone who adores you. I hope I can find someone who will adore me. My, what a wonderful feeling that must be. It's worth a half a lifetime to have someone who adores you."

"That is all she got was a half a lifetime. I know she's in heaven as she loved Jesus. The first white man she lived with taught her about the love Jesus has for us. I saw his grave and she had carved his name on a wooden cross. She told me that was what she loved him for, his love for Jesus. I wish you could have seen her face when she told me that story. It brought tears to my eyes."

"My, she was very lucky to have had two husbands she adored."

"She didn't adore her first, but she did like him very much. He traded her father two mules for her."

"My lord!" said Holley.

He never taught her English as he spoke Ute. I taught her English and how to read. We had a cabin that had many books. We both read a lot in the winter time. That cabin was much like this cabin except it had a backdoor. It set against a cliff and the backdoor opened onto a coal mine, so you didn't have to go far for your fuel. However, I like your heating system better."

"Yes, Dad was a master carpenter. He picked this place because of the hot spring. He ran pipes in the walls and ceiling to keep us warm through the winter. In the summer he had a valve that turned the water off. If he hadn't started drinking…….."

"Don't dwell on that. I know what it is to dwell on another person, and it just isn't healthy. We must live for the present. I like living with you and Elizabeth. I feel I have a family again."

Elizabeth didn't get better, as a matter of fact she became worse. In the dead of winter she passed away in her sleep."

Holley said, "What should we do. Knowing mother is gone, people will talk if we are living together."

"Well, lets bury her back of the tool shed. No one ever came to see her anyway. So who would know?"

"I guess you're right. I would hate to part from you, Alvin. I have grown quite fond of you."

"Then it's settled. If someone asked you about Elizabeth, just say that what she has may be contagious."

"My, that will keep anyone from coming up here. And we are cousins, so they think, so living together won't cause any tongues to wag."

A snow storm came that dropped six feet of snow. Alvin had bought forty bales of hay, mostly to insulate the back and side of the tool shed. Along with the twenty sacks of corn. It was enough, so they didn't have to get anymore feed for the horse that winter.

Holley couldn't leave the house as no one did unless they were completely out of food. Holley had built there food supply to a point that they had enough to last out a cold winter, so they were in good shape. No one left their houses for over two weeks.

Alvin even had stockpiled many books he had wanted to read, as Holley had warned him about being snowed in.

Gradually Alvin began to feel what Holley already felt. She said, "I hope I don't upset you Alvin, but I'm in love with you. Mother said you were the best catch I would ever get, and she was right. Don't you ever long for my arms at night, Alvin?"

"Yes, but I felt you are too young for me."

"I'm not, Alvin. I long for you at night. I want to hold you in my arms and love you. I know how Acula felt. Anyone who knew you, would feel what I do. Please sleep with me tonight."

"No, I cannot do that. We must brave the snow tomorrow and get over to Pastor Helms' parsonage. He can marry us, then we will come home. I'll make us some snow shoes tomorrow."

With Holley's help, Alvin made the snow shoes. It took an hour to go less than a half mile to Parson Helms' parsonage. He married them. His wife said, "You two must have it bad to brave this weather. How is Elizabeth holding out."

"She's braving this cold weather, Sister Lois."

That night Alvin said, "The loft or downstairs?"

"The loft. I have nearly climbed up there many nights thinking of you. You go first then I will climb that ladder like I have wanted to do for a long time."

Alvin laughed and said, "I'll be waiting."

CHAPTER 10

TROUBLE AND A TRIAL

They had latched the door, but as Alvin reached the loft, a banging came at the door. Alvin grabbed his gun and went down. He opened the door and Lon Alton fell into the cabin. Alvin did not know who he was, but knew the man was half frozen to death. He had no coat or hat. His feet were wrapped in wool clothe.

They quickly took off his clothes and wrapped him in wool blankets. While Alvin was doing that. Holley was heating some broth. She didn't even know it was her father. She thought it some stranger.

Alvin had a blanket around his head with only his mouth exposes. He was able to take the broth. After awhile he relaxed and was able to speak. He removed the blanket from his head as Holley was taking the broth back to the fire. When she turned she screamed, father! Oh my Lord, thank you Lord Jesus for returning him. He smiled and said, "I'm home, Holley. Where is Elizabeth?"

"She died Daddy just a month or two ago. I'm so sorry."

"They did this to her. She couldn't live without her man and they knew it!"

"No, Daddy, it was just her time. She was sick before you left, remember?"

"Yes, I guess I just want to blame Brunel for everything. He's been working me in that mine as a slave along with others."

Lon then looked at Alvin for the first time. He said, "Who is this, Holley?"

"He's my new husband, Alvin Scott. We were married just today."

"Where did you come from Scott?"

"I came from Indian country. I had been traveling nearly a month and Elizabeth took me in. She was so sweet to do that."

"Yeah, she would have. She had a warm heart. I will miss her. I just wish I could have been here before she passed. Damn it, I tried everything. It was this snow storm that gave me the chance. They didn't have enough guards as most of them couldn't get to the mine because of the snow. They gave us very little clothes, but the others gave what they could and I chanced it. I knew I could make it or thought I could.

"They will miss me tomorrow and will probably come for me."

"They will play hell getting here, Mr. Alton. I don't know how you made it."

"I had spotted some snow shoes and hid them knowing that sooner or later we would have a blizzard. It came and was the mother of all blizzards. It took me over an hour to get here. I just kept thinking how warm the cabin would be and kept on keeping on. If it had been another hundred feet,

I couldn't have made it. My thoughts are now, what will we do tomorrow?"

Alvin said, "I have an idea. They won't get here until around noon tomorrow. None of them know about the bathhouse. It is covered with snow. We can stock it with blankets and food. Once you're in the bathhouse, I will cover it with snow again and then cover our tracks. You should be able to last in there until they leave. Then I'll come get you."

"That sounds like a good plan. You can cover my tracks and I will just wait until you come. We had better get some sleep."

"Your bed is made, Daddy. We're sleeping in the loft."

When they were in bed, Holley said, "It kind of ruined our honeymoon, but it was worth it having daddy back."

"Well, we can wait another week until we can get away from here for a real honeymoon. Your dad will have to get out of here. I think I can get him to Steamboat Springs. He'll be safe there until we can get a U. S. Marshal up here."

The next day around noon, five men came. They came close to the door then just shot into it and yelled we know you're in there Alton. Don't make us burn you out."

What they didn't know was the shot they fired went through the door and hit Holley in the chest. She fell into Alvin's arms and passed out.

Alvin said, "I'll come out if you won't shoot. You have killed Mr. Alton's daughter."

They were shocked and said, "Come on out."

Alvin opened the door and walked out. They then rushed to the door and saw Holley lying on the floor.

Delbert yelled, "My God, what have we done."

"You've killed Holley Alton, that's what you've done. Why would you think Mr. Alton is here. He's been missing for months, I'm told."

Pete said, "Man, we are in trouble now."

Fred said, "Maybe not. We will all say that Scott killed her before we arrived. It will be five against him. Put the chains on him Paul. We'll take him back and hold him for trial. We will say that he tried to rape her and she resisted, so he shot her. We can all say she said it just before she died. He's new in town and people are really gullible. I'm sure Mr. Brunel will go along with the plan."

"Alton could never have made it here. He would have froze to death. He'll turn up next spring after the snow melts," said Delbert.

"Let's set those bales of hay afire and they will burn the cabin down and no one will find her body."

"They left with Holley's body on the floor."

Lon Alton had heard everything, but had to wait until they left. He waited until he smelled smoke then came out and saw the hay afire. He worked swiftly and pulled the burning bales away from the house. He used a pole and pushed them in one stack. They made a terrific fire and a lot of smoke. The riders who had Alvin looked back and Delbert said, "The cabin's burning."

Lon went to the house. He picked up Holey and took her to his bed. When he laid her down, she stirred. She was alive!

He donned the warmest clothes he had and dressed Holley. He picked her up and wearing his snow shoes started for Doctor Henderson's house. Although it was the nearest house to them, it was well over three hundred yards away. He went as fast as he could. He finally reached the doctor's house and kicked at the door. The doctor let him in and motioned him to a table that was padded. Lon set her down and could hear her breathing now. It was a raspy breath, but it was breath. The doctor stripped her to the waist. His wife was about to make tea, so she brought the hot water immediately. The doctor saw that the bullet had gone through her and had amazingly missed all vital organs. He cleaned the wounds thoroughly and cauterized the wounds. He said, "All we can do now is pray."

He then realized it was Lon Alton who had brought her. He said, "Where have you been, Lon?"

Brunel had me in his mine working as a slave along with several others of the town. If you can save Holley and put me up for awhile, I think we will have that rascal this time. There will be a trial. They took my new son-in-law, Alvin Scott, and will swear that he killed Holley. I heard them talking. They didn't know I was there. They think I died in the snow storm. We won't say anything until the trial is nearly over, then we'll come in and tell the court what really transpired. I heard them say that they will swear that Alvin Scott tried to rape her then shot her. I can't wait to see their faces when they see Holley and me."

"Holley is not out of the woods yet, but I think she will make it. How about a drink, Lon?"

"No, I've sworn off alcohol. I can't handle it. That is what got me in this mess in the first place."

***

Alvin was kept in the Brunel's house locked up with a twenty-four hour guard. Brunel said, "So what happened Delbert."

"We went to Alton's house and shot through the door to alarm them. I had used my fifty caliber sharp that went through the door. Then I said, 'If you don't come out, we will burn the cabin down.' Scott said, 'You've killed Holley Alton. I will come out and you can see what you've done.'"

"We were shocked to see Holley on the floor with a bullet through her chest. She was dead as a doornail. Fred here said, 'Let's all swear that Scott killed her after he tried to rape her and she confessed that before she died.'

"There was no trace of Alton. No one could make it in that snow with no shoes and very little clothing. He'll turn up next spring, and no one can prove a thing on us. That cabin had hay stacked up all around it, so we set fired to the hay and it burned the cabin down. What do you think, Boss."

"I think it's a good story, quite believable. It's unfortunate about the Alton girl, but we would have had to kill her anyway, as she would know what happened. Five against one in a court of law. They'll hang Scott and that will be that.

"We'll keep him locked up here. There is no jail in High Grove and I will bring Judge Emerson up here to see where we are keeping him. We will feed him good and let the judge make a decision on it. Since I finance his campaign each year, I'm sure he will appoint me to be Scott's custodian until the trial. I hope we can get this over in the next few weeks. I'll have Emerson hurry the trial without causing too much anxiety."

Alvin had seen Holley breath and just prayed that Lon could get her to a doctor in time. That was his only hope. He knew if they realized she was still alive, they would have to kill them both.

It took four weeks, but Holley was now on her feet and getting stronger every day. The trial was set. Everything went as Brunel had hoped. Alvin had waived a trial by jury as he knew all of Brunel's people would probably be on the jury. He just hoped that the judge would be fair. To his good luck, Judge Emerson was struck down by the flu and Judge Reynolds from Steamboat Springs was presiding. As this was a capitol case, he had brought U. S. Marshal Rex Klepper, from Denver and two of his deputies with him.

Alvin had waived his right to an attorney as the only one in town worked for Brunel and he thought he could tell a more compelling story. He knew Alton was alive even if Holley wasn't, and he counted on him coming into the courtroom near the end of the trial.

The prosecuting attorney called all five of Brunel's men to the stand and they repeated the story verbatim as they had practiced it. Alvin waited until they had all testified and then said, "Isn't it strange that each one of these men's testimony was exactly word for word the same, like they had rehearsed it for hours. It seem to me that there would be some variations."

The prosecutor said, "They simple told what happened. Scott shot the girl as they arrived. Before she died she said that Scott raped her then shot her. I will not challenge that the five men practiced their testimony, but it does not preclude that it was the truth. Nearly everyone practices what they are going to say to a court, so they get it exactly right."

Alvin then asked, Pete Copeland, who was the last to testify, "Why were you at the Alton cabin in the first place."

Pete hemmed and hawed a minute and said, "We had gotten word that Lon Alton had been seen. As he had worked for Mr. Brunel, he sent us up there to make sure Mr. Alton was okay, as he had been missing for months."

Alvin then said, "Could you tell the court why there was a bullet hole in the middle of the Alton cabin door at the precise height that the wound on Holley Alton's body is located."

The prosecutor said, "No one knows that your honor. Miss Alton's body was missing when Mr. Brunel sent the coroner to recover the body. That can be verified by the coroner who was dispatched. There is no body. Since Lon Alton was said to be seen, most people presume that he took and buried his daughter, like any father would do. Are you through with this witness, Mr. Scott?"

Alvin nodded and the prosecutor said, "I will call Mr. Brunel."

Brunel testified that he had sent the men to look in the Alton cabin to see if Mr. Alton was there. He said, "After my men made a citizen's arrest of Scott, I brought Judge Emerson to my house to see that the prisoner was properly housed and feed. I was appointed the custodian of Mr. Scott until the trial. I have fulfilled my duty."

The prosecutor then said, "You may step down Mr. Brunel."

Alvin then said, "Just a minute, I have some questions for Mr. Brunel."

The judge said, "You may proceed Mr. Scott."

Mr. Brunel, "Is it true that you kept Mr. Alton and several towns people in your mine as slave laborers?"

Before he could answer, the prosecutor said, "This has nothing to do with the case at hand and I ask that the question be denied by the court."

Alvin said, "You're the one who said that Mr. Brunel was looking for Mr. Alton, as he said someone had seen him and you wanted to know if he was okay. I contend that Mr. Brunel knew that Mr. Alton had escaped and his five henchmen were looking to bring him back or kill him, so I think the question pertinent."

The Judge said, "I will allow the question as you, Mr. Prosecutor, brought Mr. Alton into the case as evidence."

Brunel said, "I certainly did not know anything about Mr. Alton and was only concerned with his welfare."

"If that is true, Mr. Brunel, will you object to the U. S. Marshal searching your mine after the trial?" Brunel was sweating now and said, "Of course he can, I have nothing to hide."

At that time Pastor Helms came into the courtroom and went straight to Alvin's table and whispered. "When do want your witnesses. Holley is alive and wants to testify. Her father is also outside and ready to testify."

Alvin then addressed the court and said, "Your honor, will you order the search of Mr. Brunel's mine immediately after the trial, and order the five men who testified to stay with the marshal until the search is made?"

"I will order the search, as Mr. Brunel has specified that he has no objection, and I will order the five men who work for Mr. Brunel, to stay with the marshal."

"Does the prosecution rest its case, Mr. Prosecutor?"

"Yes, your honor."

"Does the defendant have any witnesses, Mr. Scott?"

"Scott said, "I do your honor. I call Pastor Helms.""

Pastor Helms was at Alvin's table and took the stand. After he was sworn in, Alvin asked, "Pastor Helms, did you perform a marriage ceremony about four weeks ago?"

"Yes, I married you to Holley Alton."

The courtroom gasped and began talking. Judge Reynolds banged his gavel and said "Order in the court," and everyone became quiet.

"I might ask your honor, does it sound highly illogical that a husband would attempt to rape his wife on the second day of their marriage?"

"I'm not here to make conjecture, Mr. Scott, but nearly anyone would assume he wouldn't."

"Then I contend that the five men, who testified to that end, perjured themselves, as each one said I did, as they all said the same thing, verbatim."

The prosecutor said, "That is a judgment that the court must decide at another hearing. It does not pertain to this case."

"I contend it does pertain to this case, as these men are either credible witnesses or they're liars."

Judge Reynolds said, "I will take that into consideration in my decision."

Alvin then said, "I call Lon Alton to the stand." Again there was a buzz in the audience and Judge Reynolds hit his gavel and it stopped, as Lon walked to the stand and was sworn in. Alvin then said, "Mr. Alton, were you present when the five men who testified came to your cabin around noon on the fourteenth of last month.?"

Alton answered, "I was. I was in a bathhouse I built near the spring which is just steps from the front door of my cabin.

It was hidden from view as it was covered by snow. I didn't see the men, but I knew it was the five, as I knew their voices."

"Will you tell the court what was said?"

"They were yelling for me to come out of the cabin. They said that if I didn't, they would burn down the cabin. One of them then shot through the door with his rifle. I didn't see who did it, but after they left, I could see the hole and my daughter lying on the floor of the cabin. They had set fire to the bales of hay that were stacked against the walls of the cabin. I first pulled all the burning bales of hay away from the cabin then pushed them into one place, so the fire would look like the cabin was burning if they looked back."

The prosecutor said, "I contend that what this witness has said is hearsay, as he did not see the men."

Alvin said, "I was a witness to all this and what Mr. Alton said, is true. If it wasn't them, who took me into custody?" The prosecutor had no answer and sat down.

The judge said, "I will rule that the five men who testified were the men who Mr. Alton heard talking."

The prosecutor said, "How do we know that Mr. Alton and Mr. Scott didn't conspirer with that answer?"

Alvin said, "Because we never saw each other after they took me. I was in Brunel's custody against my will."

The judge said, "My ruling stands."

"What did you do after the men left, Mr. Alton?" Alvin asked.

"I picked up Holley and could tell she was alive, so I rushed her to Doc Henderson's house. He worked on her for an hour and told me she would probably live."

"Well, did she survive?" asked Alvin

"Yes, and she is outside ready to testify." and again the courtroom was alive with conversation. The judge again hit his gavel and the courtroom quieted.

Brunel's face was pale as he realized he was about to be arrested.

The prosecutor could now tell it was useless to proceed as there was no murder if Holley Alton Scott was present.

Alvin then said, "I call Holley Scott to the stand." As she walked in, the prosecutor said, "I concede the case and drop all charges against Mr. Scott."

Alvin said, "As Mr. Brunel held me against my will, knowing I was innocent, I contend he is guilty of kidnapping. I also contend that he held Mr. Alton against his will as well as other towns people, and should be arrested on multiple charges of kidnapping.

"I also, would like to bring charges against the five witness for perjury, shooting Mrs. Scott and conspiring with Mr. Brunel in the kidnapping."

"I will do that, Mr. Scott. Bailiff put handcuffs on all six of these men. Marshal Klepper, arrest these men and take them to the jail in Steamboat Springs for prosecution."

The six men were taken in a coach to Steamboat Springs and kept in custody there. Brunel's mine was searched and three others including the editor of the paper were found and released. The mine was immediately shut down and most of the men in High Grove were now out of work."

Alvin went to Judge Emerson, who had now lost his monthly payoff from Brunel, and asked, "Would you appoint me as custodian of the mine until the court can decide who is now the owner of Brunel's mine? Half of High Grove's men need to go back to work. There families will really suffer unless the mine is reopened."

The judge thought awhile and said, "I could do that, but you will need advice from time to time. Would you use me as your attorney?"

Alvin could see the judge was a conniver and said, "I will do that, unless your fees are out of line."

The mine was reopened and now Alvin was the acting owner. He brought Holley into the office to help. He hired Lon Alton to run the operating end."

CHAPTER 11

DEADLY TROUBLE

Brunel's lawyer came to see him in the Steamboat jail. Brunel said, "You remember Cal Hansen." The lawyer nodded and Brunel said, "He has a cabin here. Have him come see me. Now, he won't be able to see me alone unless he is wearing a suit and tie and has a briefcase. He can tell the guard he has to counsel with me about my up coming trial. The guard will think he's a lawyer and let him in."

Don't tell me the details Martin. I'll give him your message."

Cal came the next day. He was groomed and in a suit and tie with a briefcase. The guard let him in and left as prisoners were allowed to be alone with their lawyers.

Brunel said, "I have a considerable amount of money in various banks, so you know I'm good for a payoff. I'll pay you five hundred dollars to follow this plan. Get your boys together, then send a note to the jail that says to bring me to Judge Reynolds' chambers as he wants to talk with me. You wear a deputy sheriff's badge and wait for the deputy to bring me out of the jail. When you see him with me, give your men the high sign to start shooting at one another like it's a gunfight with the law. That's when your boy, Mark, runs up and tells the deputy that the marshal wants him up there to help him, because he has two of the Blanton gang cornered. Tell him you will take the prisoner back to jail, until the shootings is over. He may argue, but your boy can tell him the marshal was insistent that he come. He will turn me over to you and go up the street. You can be watching and when we leave, wait until just before we cut into the alley and then give the boys the high sign. They will disburse and Mark can put me in a buggy. Have a frock coat ready for me, a scarf to put around my throat and face, and a top hat. Have Martha Jane in the buggy in her best outfit and we will ride out of town.

"Can you handle it?"

"Nothing to it, boss. Where will we meet?"

"At the hideout near Medicine Rock."

The plan was put in motion and came off just like it was planned. At the hideout, Brunel said, "Martha Jane and I are going to Denver. I want you to go to High Grove and stake out that cabin that Alton and his daughter live in. I want you to wait until they are in the cabin then break in the door and throw enough dynamite in the door to blow anyone in the cabin to smithereens. Can you do that?"

"I need to know what's in it for the boys?"

"Two hundred dollars each. Plus another two hundred for you. I'll meet you all in Denver and pay you off, you know the place. Then we'll have a party."

"Sounds like a winner, Boss."

"Two of Cal's men rode into High Grove. It was about six in the evening and they got directions to Alton's cabin. Alton,

Holley and Alvin had come from work. When they arrived. Alvin said, "I was in the mine all day, and have dirt all over me, as I was investigating a new seam that seems to have a great deal of gold in it. I want to bathe and put on some clean clothes."

Alvin took his valise with him that had nearly everything he owned in it. He always took his guns with him.

He had just got into the water to soak when Cal and his men rode up. Alvin heard the riders and began to dry up and put on his clothes. He was just about dressed when he heard a tremendous explosion that shook the bathhouse violently. When he recovered, he ran to the cabin, as the men were riding off.

The door of the cabin was blown off. He lit a match as the lamps had been destroyed and smoke inundated the room. He could see that both Holley and Lon were dead and the cabin's inside destroyed. Part of the roof was gone also. There were still small fires around the cabin burning from the blast. He used a blanket and smothered them out.

He ran back to the bathhouse where he had a lamp. He brought it into the cabin and could see the mangled bodies of both Holley and Lon.

He went to the tool house and his horse was shaken, but okay. He saddled and rode to get Bill Owens at his furniture store. Bill acted as the undertaker for the town. He explained what had happened. Bill got some men and they left to take care of the bodies.

Alvin was devastated. He thought, *"I will never marry again. Everyone of them die after we are married. No, I will never subject any woman to this again. I wonder what I've done to make God so angry at me?"*

He retrieved his valise and went to the hotel for the night.

There were many at the funeral. No one tried to comfort Alvin, as they could see this would be impossible. As they were leaving the graveyard, Alvin told Judge Emerson that he could not carry on at the mine and that he needed to appoint someone else to manager the mine.

"Where will you go, Alvin?"

"I don't know, but it will be away from here. I'm leaving right now."

He rode to Steamboat Springs as the railroad had completed the line to there. He sold his horse and took the train to Denver.

Gene Carne was glad to see him. He brought him up to date on how the hotel was doing. Gene said, "I told you this was a goldmine. I love running it. You would think it would be work, but I enjoy everything I do, even settling customer's gripes."

"It must be great when you find your niche in life, Gene. I have the mine, but I have a partner in that, too. He enjoys mining like you do the hotel. I just hope I can find something that I like to do."

Gene said, "By the way, where is Acula?"

"It's a sad tale, Gene. The Indians killed her. I was standing right beside her and a bullet took her, but left me alive. I was able to get away from the Indians only because a terrific hail storm arrived."

"The Lord moves in mysterious ways, Alvin. I know he has something for you to do, yet, or he would have taken you, too. I am sorry to hear about her. She was a happy person. I noticed how she adored you."

"Yes, and I her. It left a hollow place in my life, I can never fill."

"Don't say "never," Alvin. The Lord can fill that place left by Acula. I have learned to depend on him for everything I do. He has brought me to the place that I feel I can't do nothing without his guidance. My wife helped me to realize that."

"Well, I had better get out to the mine and see Jake and Maria. I have been gone over a year now. They have probably started a city out at the mine." Alvin was just kidding, as he thought about the two houses that had been built.

When he arrived, the place was a city. He was amazed at the number of houses. There were streets and several stores. Alvin had no idea what had transpired since he had gone. Jake had an operation that was now, a commercial mine.

Jake and Maria were both glad to see him. They were very sad to hear about Acula. Jake told him how he had increased the size of the mining operation. He said, "Alvin have you checked our account at the bank?"

"No, but I will when I return. Are we rich?" Rich enough that I propose selling the mine. I have been offered two million dollars for it. I would like to sell it before the ore runs out. We have enough money to last us many life times. What do you say?"

"I say 'sell,' You know more about this than I ever would. I think I'm leaving this area for a spell. I think I'll explore California and possibly Oregon and Washington. I hope to catch the transcontinental railroad to San Francisco then go by ship north."

"Well, good luck, Alvin. You are the best friend I ever had. I would say that if we had run out of gold the first week. I shall miss Acula, also."

They parted and Alvin went back to Denver.

As Alvin was walking from a livery stable to the hotel he saw Brunel going into a tavern. It shocked him, but he knew it was him. He went straight to Marshal Klepper's office and told him he had just seen Martin Brunel going into a tavern. Klepper had three men go with him. One of his men named, Lively, said, "How long ago did you see him?"

"About five to ten minutes ago. He was going into that tavern on Fifth Street, next to the Post Office."

Lively yelled at two deputies that were at the back of the office. Both had been with Klepper in High Grove at the trial. They all grabbed shotguns and the four left with Alvin trailing them. Klepper and two of the deputies went into the tavern while one of them covered the front door. Alvin went around to the back alley to cover the backdoor.

Sheriff Klepper spotted the men and went straight to the back. Brunel saw them coming and turned over the table and said, "Shoot! It's a raid!"

Two of the outlaws saw they didn't have much of a chance against shotguns and stood and raised their hands, but Cal and those that were in on killing Alton and Holley, began shooting.

Just after Brunel turned over the table he scooted under another table and headed for the back door, while the rage of battle was going on. He reached the backdoor and opened it and stepped out into the alley. Alvin was waiting beside the door and put a pistol to his head and said, "Just one wrong move, and I'll blow your head off."

Brunel knew he was caught dead to rights and put up no fight, and walked meekly around the building to the front of the tavern. When he got there, Marshal Klepper was coming out with the two who had raised their hands.

Klepper had a superficial wound on the side of his face and one of his deputies had a shoulder wound.

Klepper said, "I see you got Brunel."

"Yeah, he was trying to slip out the backdoor, but I was covering it."

"The other's are dead. We cut them in half with our shotguns."

He turned to Brunel and said, "Now, we can add the count of first degree murder to your rap sheet."

Alvin said, "I hope he doesn't get the death penalty, I would like to know he is working at hard labor the rest of his life. I thought about shooting him in the knee, but then he wouldn't be able to work until he dies."

Klepper said, "Either way, society will be rid of another rat. Hey, Lively, you best get on to the hospital, we can handle these yahoos."

"How about you, Marshal?"

"That's just a little scratch. It will make me look meaner," and they all laughed.

Alvin waited until after the trial. Brunel escaped the death penalty, but was sentenced to life at hard labor.

Four months later, Alvin was on a train headed for San Francisco.

CHAPTER 12

THE TRAIN RIDE

Alvin caught the train headed for San Francisco from Cheyenne. He had his bank in Denver transfer a hundred thousand dollars to the Bank of San Francisco. His banker in Denver knew the owner of that bank and highly recommended him.

Alvin took a thousand dollars with him. He had a gunsmith bore a hole in his rifle butt near the place that held the extra tube. The hole was then sealed with a wooden plug.

He kept three hundred dollars in his wallet and carried fifty dollars in coins in his pocket. He put the remainder of his thousand dollars in the hole that was drilled. He felt relatively safe, but you never knew what circumstances could occur.

That evening he went to the dining car and it was full except for a seat across from a lady. Alvin approached her and asked, "Would you mind if I sat with you for dinner?" She put on a beautiful smile and said, "I would be delighted."

The waiter was a long time getting to them so Alvin said, "I'm Alvin Scott from Denver."

She said, "I'm Mrs. Gerald Wilson, from Philadelphia. I'm on my way to Carson City to join my husband, who has recently been appointed as the director of the mint there. He went before me as the director there had a stroke, and is incapacitated. They needed Mr. Wilson there as soon as he could get there. I had to close up the house and conclude our business before following him."

The waiter came and handed them a menu. They both ordered the roast beef.

Alvin said to Mrs. Wilson, "Would you have a glass of wine with me?"

"Yes, that would be nice. You choose it, as I am not too familiar with wine. My husband is against all alcohol. However, I always liked wine with my meals as my family nearly always had it at dinner, and I miss it."

"Do you have a merlot?" Alvin asked the waiter.

"We have a merlot from the Napa Valley, Sir."

"Please bring us a bottle."

When the waiter left them, Alvin said, "Your husband must be well thought of to be appointed as the director. You must be quite proud of him."

"Actually, he was in line for the promotion as he has been with the mint for twenty-five years."

This shocked Alvin as Mrs. Wilson was obviously in her late twenties. However, many men married younger women if their first wife passed away.

Mrs. Wilson could tell Alvin was uneasy with her remark, so she said, "I'm Mr. Wilson's second wife. His first wife was taken by the Spanish flu. Our families were close and could see Gerald needed someone badly. He is such a good man that at my father's urging, I married him. He has two grown children, who resent me, so I was quite pleased with the move." She then flushed and said, "I don't know what came over me to tell you these things. We just met."

"I took it as an honor that you would confide in me. I will tell you something about myself so you won't feel badly. I have been married twice. Both of my wives were killed. One by Indians and the other by an explosion set to kill her and me, but I was in a bathhouse near our cabin and was not injured. My first wife was killed as we stood shoulder to shoulder. A bullet knocked me down, saving me, but my wife was taken by a hail of bullets. I have decided to never marry again as it appears that anyone who loves me, ends up tragically."

"My!" Mrs. Wilson said, "I am so sorry. You are such a nice man, I wish I could do something to alleviate your pain."

"That is very nice of you, Mrs. Wilson, but no one can help me, but time. I will never allow any woman to love me again."

Alvin could see the painful expression on Mrs. Wilson's face as she sympathized with him. He then said, "Don't take on my grief, Mrs. Wilson. I wanted to make you feel better, but I see I did the opposite."

"Yes, but we now have a bond between us. In my position, close friends are hard to come by as you never know who you can trust. In just two or three minutes we have become very close knowing each of our inner most secrets. I feel very fortunate to have met you Mr. Scott."

"If we are that close, you must call me Alvin."

"Then you can call me Cara. It makes the trip so much better, having a close friend to talk with. Please tell me something about your wives, Alvin. I want to know them."

"My first wife was half Indian. She kept me from dying. I was in the army and the Indians ambushed our patrol and killed everyone but me. I was shot in the shoulder and a bullet hit the edge of my skull and rendered me uncurious. Cuela, was watching the battle transpire as she was hiding from the Indians. She checked each body after the Indians left, and I was still alive, so she took me to a cave she was staying in. She nursed me back to health. I just tolerated her at first, but then because of her kindness began to like her, then like turned to love as I got to know her. I can still see those adoring eyes when she looked at me. After she was killed, I felt I could never love another woman like I loved her. However, I made my way to a town in Colorado and stayed with a family there.

"Holley, my next wife lived there. Her mother actually took me in as her husband had been kidnapped, and put to work in a mine as a slave laborer. The mother died a few months later. Their daughter, who was only nineteen, had fallen in love with me. Probably because of loneliness. Although I didn't love her as I had Cuela, I did love her. As her mother had died, it would have been improper to stay together, unwed, in that cabin, so I married her. However, not long after our marriage, she was killed in a terrible dynamite blast."

"I see you as the most loving man I have ever known. Tell me more about Cuela. You were probably isolated from people. How did you communicate."

We spent hours during the winter teaching each other our languages. I taught her to read and she became quite proficient at it. We had many books.

"When she was fifteen, her father took her and her sister to a place where the Indians met with trappers and miners once a year to trade. He traded her for two mules to a white man. He was a middle-aged mountain man who was very clever. He built a cabin that was hidden. He was an expert carpenter and they lived very well. He knew the Ute language and never taught Cuela English. Some years later, he was killed by Indians.

Cuela went back to live with her father. However, her father had been killed, and she lived alone in his tepee. A warrior became keen on her and came to her tepee one evening and began to rape her. Her yells brought the warrior's wife. Instead of blaming her husband, she had Cuela kicked out of the tribe. She had been out of the tribe only a few weeks until she found me.

"Cuela took me back to the trappers cabin and we lived there about three years. One day when I was washing our eating utensils in a stream next to us, I discovered gold in the stream. It made us very wealthy. I tried to take Cuela to Europe, but she wanted to explore the wilds. She loved nature. So we picked up and went west over the Rocky Mountains. That's where we had Indian trouble and she was killed. I don't regret a moment with Cuela. I don't know how to explain it, but when someone adores you, it is something that is almost holy. She loved our Lord, Jesus as I do, so I know she is in heaven."

"Although your story is tragic, you are a very lucky man. You had someone that adored you. Oh, what a feeling."

Their meal arrived and they ate in silence. They drank all of the wine. After the meal Cara said, "The seat beside me is empty. Will you sit by me?"

They had just sat down when the train jumped the rails and wrecked badly. The engine descended a steep grade and had picked up considerable speed. It came to a curve where the rail had been broken loose from the ties. It sent the train into a canyon pulling all the cars with it. The train consisted of an engine, coal car, baggage car, two passenger cars and the caboose. The engine raced down into the canyon turning over on its side with the coal car. The baggage car had broken loose from the coal car and raced up the small canyon to a flat place. It slide against the bank slowing it down and preventing it from toppling over.

The two passenger cars broke loose from the baggage car and slide on their sides following the engine and coal car. Although on their side, the two passenger cars and the caboose slide to a sudden stop that jettisoned the passenger forward. All that saved Alvin and Cara was they were at the last seat in front and the area in front of them next to the end of the car was filled with bags of the passengers. This cushioned them although they were bruised considerably.

Some of the people went over them and hit the front wall of the car. Neither Alvin and Cara became unconscious, although they were bruised and hurt. Alvin thought it miraculous that no bones were broken. The other passengers had been ejected from their seats and sent airborne against the front wall. Bodies then came down on Alvin and Cara burying them in bodies. Alvin wormed his way out as did Cara. They were now standing on the side of the car against the ground. All of the windows had shattered or cracked badly.

Although late in the afternoon, there was still considerable light. The first thing Alvin thought of was the fire in the stove that had been hurled like the passengers forward. The fire was scattered and Alvin quickly put out the flames before they could ignite the car.

Out of the heap of passengers they heard two people moaning. It was two women who were in the heap of bodies. They managed to pull them out and although shaken and bruised, appeared to be okay. Looking at the other passengers they could tell most were dead and if not dead, unconscious.

Alvin then smelled smoke. He quickly looked around, but it was not coming from their car. It was from the passenger car that had come to rest on top of a portion of their car. Alvin went to a window and looked out. The other passenger car was in flames. He realized that the fire from the other coach would soon spread to their coach, and knew they must get out quickly.

Alvin said to the women, "The other coach is in flames and will soon spread to our coach. We must get out as soon as we can. We have a little time. Find your baggage and dress as warmly as you can for we will be outside."

He then checked the doors on each end of the coach. They were still in tack, but were jammed together making them impossible to access. Most of the windows were broken. He told Cara to put on her warmest clothing, because they would probably be outside for a long time and it was getting colder.

Cara, then and there, decided she would do everything Alvin said, without question. Throwing inhabitation to the wind she redressed herself and put on her long underwear then her wool slacks, then her wool sweater. She had a heavy coat and put it on. She also had some earmuffs that she put on. While she was doing this, Alvin changed his clothes as did the two women. He was already in his wool long johns, but he put on a wool, shirt, a sweater and his buckskins over that. He also had a warm wool coat and put that on. He looked around and found his rifle, and opened his valise and strapped on his scabbard and pistol.

He found a window that was completely broken and by stepping on the broken seats the women could get out the window with his help. He pulled himself out first and then reached down and caught Cara by the wrist and lifted her up onto the top of the car that was on its side. He put his hand back down and caught the wrist or the next woman and pulled her out easily. The other woman put her hand up, but she weighed a lot more and he barely was able to pull her through the window. By now the flames were leaping onto their coach and it was being filled with smoke. He looked back in the car and nothing was stirring. He knew some of them were probably alive, but with the flames coming, he could do nothing about it.

They heard screams coming from the other coach as it was now completely covered in flames. It was getting dusk and Alvin knew they were in for a cold night. The wind was blowing hard and taking the flames from the coach, that was completely in flames, to their coach. He went to the end of the car, away from the flames, and was able to make his way down to the ground. The women followed him and he was able to assist them to the ground. They then moved away from the coach, because flames began to consume their coach and spread to the caboose.

The four backed away from the flames. They were not too far away from the stream that was tuning into a river. As the women looked at the flame, Alvin began to go toward the front of the train. He saw the baggage car about a hundred feet ahead of him. It was sitting upright on a flat piece of ground not too far from the stream, but close to a bluff. He thought the baggage car was far enough away that it would not catch fire.

He then felt the first drops of a rain. He walked further and could see that the engine was on its side. He surmised that the engineer and the fireman were both dead as he could find neither.

By this time it was beginning to rain. He moved back to the women and said, "We need to take shelter. The only place I see to get out of the weather is that baggage car." and he pointed and they followed him.

As they walked, Alvin thought, *"It is miraculous that that car is up right. The bank must have kept it upright."* It was damaged some, but not that badly. Alvin was able to open the door. He pulled himself up, then turned and pulled the women into the car. Once inside one of the women found a kerosene lantern and turned it upright and lit it giving them some light. That light enabled them to find other lanterns.

The light showed them a man who was lying on the floor. Alvin checked him. He was dead. He had hit his head on the corner of a safe that was there and crushed his skull. Alvin put him at the head of the car where he saw a stack of blankets. He put one over the man.

While he was doing that, Cara and one of the women had put the stove back on its base. To their good fortune, the stove had not been lit. They found a coal supply and made a fire. They then rummaged around looking for anything that may help. One of the women found a storage bin that had been built onto the side of the car. It contained provisions and many other items. One of them was a coffee pot.

The storm outside was now raging. The rain was a deluge. Cara went over and opened the boxcar door a crack. She could see water running off the roof and held the coffee pot in the stream of water until the coffee pot was full. She then put the pot on top of the stove that had a flat surface. One of the women then put coffee in the pot.

Each of them took a blanket and sat around the stove. One of the women said, "I'm Doris Singleton and this is my sister, Martha." Looking at Alvin she said, "What are we going to do?"

"The first thing I'm going to do is to find some raingear. I noticed this car is not far above that stream outside. If this rain increases it could fill this canyon and we could drown. The steel trucks on this car are so heavy they it may keep the car in place, but the water will come in and drown us. I'm not trying to scare you, I'm just telling you the facts. You must listen to me and carry out my orders without question. It's the only way you will survive."

The women all knew the situation was dire, and were grateful they had Alvin to lead them. After sometime he found the raingear of the man who tended the baggage car. He drank some coffee first, sharing a cup with Cara as she handed it to him. Reluctantly, he opened the boxcar door and surveyed the area. There was still some light. He could see the stream of water and could tell it had grown considerably since they had reached the car. He could even tell by the sound of the rush of water that it was growing steadily.

He hopped down onto the ground and began to survey the bank of the canyon. He could tell somewhat where the high water mark was, but knew that the water could exceed this the way the rain was coming down. He walked up the bank and found a shelf against another cliff. It had an overhang. It jutted out so that there was a recess where the rain and most of the wind were kept out. He investigated it and knew this was the place they must go if the water continued to rise.

He went back to the car and banged on it until one of the women opened it. He pulled himself in and closed the door. He then reported what he had found. He said, "The other door is against the bank so it can't be used, so we must use this door."

The stove had heated the car some and Cara handed him a cup of coffee. Alvin said, "One of us has to monitor that stream and make sure we have time to get away before the water is high enough to get us wet. I have a pocket watch and will have each of us watch the water for an hour, then wake the other."

Martha said, "I will take the first watch, then I will wake, Doris. She can wake Cara and she can wake you." They each then rolled up in their blankets and went to sleep.

During the second watch, Doris fell asleep. Alvin was awakened by cold water on his leg. He then could feel that the car was awash with water. He knew that the stream had become a river and that the boxcar would soon be inundated with water. He yelled at the others and said, "We must leave now, because the water is going to fill the car. We've got to get to a place and get out of the water or we'll all drown."

Alvin then opened the door a bit and could tell there was a raging river and the water was rising. By now, the water was up to their ankles. It was hard to keep their balance because the car was now rocking from the water hitting it. They had to keep hold of something or fall down.

Alvin had his rifle in his hand. He turned to Cara and said, "We need to go now before the water gets deeper. Can you swim?"

"Yes," Cara said.

Both Martha and Doris said, "We can't swim, what will we do?"

"Grab something that will float and hang onto it."

It was so dark they couldn't see very far outside the car. They could hear the raging water. It was then the car began to get deeper and Alvin said, "We must go now."

Alvin waited until he saw a tree coming and told Doris and Martha to jump onto that tree and they may make it. They both jumped as they minded Alvin and knew he was giving them their only chance. They both made it, and the last Alvin and Cara saw of them, they were clinging to that tree. They were quickly out of sight.

Alvin had told Cara to hang onto his rifle barrel with both hands as long as she could. They then jumped and were swirling downstream. Trees were in the water and Alvin just knew they would be crushed.

He saw a huge tree coming their way and said, "Try to get onto that tree as it passes, we may be able to stay with it long enough to get to shore."

The tree was there and they both caught it, and were able to hold on to it. It washed near shore minutes later. They were both clinging to the shore side of the tree. Alvin said, "Jump for shore, I think we can make it."

They jumped and partially swam and waded until they were both on land. It was still raining. Alvin noticed she had never let go of his rifle. They were drenched, but had all their clothes and shoes on. Alvin put out his free hand and said, "There is a cliff over there, I think. We may find shelter there."

With extreme difficulty they made their way to the cliff. They found an overhang and below it was dry. However, their clothes were soaking wet. They took off their coats and wrung them out as best they could. They were both freezing. Alvin just knew they would freeze to death unless he could find a cave or a recess in the cliff where he could build a fire.

Alvin bent down and above the sound of the wind, rushing water and rain said, "I've got to find us someplace where I can build a fire or we'll die. I'll be back soon, just wrap up in our coats until I get back."

She looked at him and said, "If I die, know that I love you."

Alvin smiled and said, "I'll be back."

He left and was walking at the edge of the cliff. It was difficult as large rocks were everywhere. He came to a wooded area that had trees right up to the bluff. It was now getting lighter. He knew if he went into the trees it would get darker, but he went anyway. His teeth were chattering and he was cold to the bone.

As it got lighter, he saw a cave. He looked at it, and it was just what he had wanted. He went back and got Cara. They made their way to the cave. It was now light enough to see clearly.

Inside the cave was a place where others had built fires. He could see where packrats had built nests and there was a lot of firewood that someone had brought in. He gathered the tender from the rats nests and then took one of his cartridges from his belt and used his pocketknife and cut the lead loose. He did this with several of his bullets. He then found some flint and used the barrel of his pistol to create a spark that immediately burst the gunpowder into flames. He added small sticks and then some of the wood that someone had provided. Soon he had a roaring fire.

With some of the branches, he was able to put up a tripod to hang their coats on. He turned to Cara and said, "We'll let our coats dry some, then we must take off our clothes and dry them."

It was a long process, but just before they ran out of wood, their clothes were dry. Alvin then said, "We need more wood. It's quit raining so I will look along the cliff and see if I can find some dry wood."

He was gone a long time, but she could hear him coming dragging a small tree. She came out and helped him drag it into the cave. They broke off the limbs and were able to rekindle the fire. He then drug the log into the flames until it too, was burning.

Cara said, "I wonder if Doris and Martha made it?"

"Not much of a chance. They will probably make it to shore, but if they do they have no way of getting warm and will probably die of exposure. Doris did us in by falling asleep. She just didn't know the seriousness of our dilemma and it cost both their lives, too, bad."

"We've got to go now. We have no food and are some distance from the tracks. We will follow the river back to where the tracks are."

Cara said, "I'll feel better when we get back to the train. The engine and coal car can't wash away and someone will come to see what happened to the train sooner or later."

"If it starts to snow, it will be bad."

It did start to snow. They had been traveling for over an hours and Cara said, "I can't go any further. Go on without me, you can make it."

"I don't want to make it without you. I couldn't live with myself."

Cara came into his arms and said, "I love you. You're the first man I ever loved. I married out of obligation, but I love you."

"Most of your love is gratitude. You don't realize it now, but it is."

"No, I know I love you, that will never change."

"Don't love me. Every woman who does, dies."

"Yes, but none of them would want to live without you. I see what they saw. Even if I die, I want to be with you."

"Well, come on then. We've got to go on. We don't want to die here."

"Okay, but you'll have to give me some help."

An hour before dark they had reached the train. The water had receded and the engine and coal car were out of water, but on their sides. The coal had come out of the coal car and left a place where they could hole up out of the weather.

Alvin said, "At least we will have plenty of fuel. Maybe the engineer and fireman have some grub stashed away."

He went to the engine and sure enough, he found quite a lot of food. It had been kept dry as the engineer had put the food in a large tin bread box to keep it fresh. He also found a coffee pot and a can of coffee. Alvin started a fire and soon they were fed again and were drinking hot coffee.

They were somewhat warm as the fire reflected off the steel side of the coal car and kept them warm. It was now snowing steadily outside. Cara cuddled up to Alvin and kissed him. He smiled at her and said, "What would your husband say."

"I don't care, I love you. If we make it through this, take me to that cabin you and Cuela lived in."

"It's not there anymore. The mine took it. There is a city there now with probably two hundred people."

"How about the cabin that was partially blown up. Could you fix it?"

"I could do that, but I don't want to live in High Grove. It's a small mining town that has nothing to offer. No, I would want more. I was heading for San Francisco and then maybe north to Alaska, visiting all the places. Cuela wanted to see those places."

"Are you telling me that you don't want me?"

"Perhaps. Everyone who links up with me dies a tragic death. I don't want that to happen to you."

"I'll chance it."

"If you are serious, I think you should go to Carson City and tell your husband that your life has changed, and you can no longer be with him. Tell him it has nothing to do with him, but nearly losing your life has changed your whole perception of life. Then write your parents, and tell them you can no longer live with Gerald Wilson. Say you are going to California to redefine yourself."

The next day a work train came and rescued them. They were taken to Ogdon on another train. They parted at Fallon,

Nevada and Cara said she would meet him at his hotel in San Francisco. Alvin took his rifle and took the wooden plug out and withdrew the tube with the money in it.

Cara said, "Now I see why you held onto that rifle for dear life." Alvin smiled and gave her three-hundred dollars incase Gerald became stingy and would not give her any money.

Wilson was just that. He said, "You're going back home to meet your lover. I saw Hawkins looking at you."

"No, I'm not going home. I'm going to San Francisco and from there I might go north to Alaska. I need a whole new prospective of life. I don't love you and never did. I felt sorry for you when Wanda died, and that seemed to turn into something it shouldn't have."

"It's because of my selfish children. They always resented you. I could see it. Well, they won't do that again, I promise."

"It's not that Gerald. I don't love you, and can't stay with you. I want to start a new life and have a new beginning."

"On what? You have no money."

"I have some savings and I can live on that until I find work. I want to be on my own."

"Go and be damned. You'll not get a cent from me. You will probably have to whore for a living. You probably will like that work. So go, I don't want to ever see you again."

CHAPTER 13

THE RESCUE OF THE WOMEN

Two cowboys were quartered in a line shack not too far from the stream next to the track. They were eating their supper and one of they said, "You know, that stream can become a river. There are several cows with small calves. The cows are smart enough to stay away from the stream, but if a wall of water came through while they were getting water, some of them may be swept away. Let's put on our raingear, saddle up and ride down there and watch for awhile."

Hank said, "We have nothing else to do. I would like to see how high that stream rises."

They saddled up and rode to a high bank of the raging water and readied their ropes just incase they saw a cow or a calf. They had not sat there very long until they heard the shout of a woman. They then saw the two women coming that were clinging to a tree.

They both threw their lassos and roped both women. The women immediately let loose the tree. The men tying their ropes to the saddle horn, backed their horses, and dragged the two women up onto the bank. They then got off their horses and ran toward the women. They took the ropes off them and picked them up and took them to their horse, and carried them to their line shack.

Both Tex and Hank knew the women were near hypothermia, but knew just what to do. They first sat them in a chair. They unlaced their shoes and pulled off their shoes and socks. They then pulled off their coats and started undoing their dresses. They took every stitch of clothes they had on off. They then put blankets over them.

The women just sat and tried to help them undress them, but their hands would not function because they were too cold. Wool socks were then brought. Both men had another set of long johns and put these on the women. After that Tex brought them a cup of coffee that was heavily laced with whiskey. Everything until then was done in silence.

Martha managed to speak and said, "You saved our lives, thank you."

After the women drank the coffee the men picked them up and put them in their bunk beds, then laid the blankets over them. They were so exhausted they were asleep in seconds.

Tex then poured them each a cup of coffee and said, "Those are the two prettiest redheads I ever seen. God just dropped them out of the sky for us to rope. I wonder where they came from to be in that water. I believe it was God who brought us to that bank. Just think, they were over thirty feet from us, and we both made a perfect throw. I say it was God who did that, too."

I think you're right, Tex. We are just two dumb cowboys who never did anything in our lives but tend cows, until tonight. We must listen to God more carefully, Tex. He really spoke to us tonight."

"They are beautiful, Hank and to think, God chose us to rescue them. I can't wait to talk to them."

They then got more blankets and made themselves bedrolls and went to sleep on the floor. The next morning, both men were up early and made flapjacks for the women. The women then arose in their long johns and Doris said, "Do you have a bathroom?"

Tex grinned and said, "Yes and no. We have an outhouse. You need to get on your shoes and put your coats on. You'll see it off to the left as you go out the door."

"Both women put on their shoes and coats and left. While they were gone, Tex found a couple of boxes and drew them up to the table with the chairs so everyone would have a seat. The flapjacks were ready and Hank brought a jug of sorghum to put on them.

Tex poured each a cup of coffee.

The girls returned and took off their coats. They saw that the men had made a clothesline with their ropes and hung all their clothes to dry. Martha felt the clothes and they were still damp.

She turned to the men and said, "Since you've already seen all that we have, I hope you won't be embarrassed if we eat in your underwear."

Tex said, "Ma'am, don't think nothing about us seeing you nude. We took it as if you were just a couple of calves that needed tending to."

Doris looked at Martha and said, "Being compared to calves is a real compliment, he could have said hogs."

Tex said, "We didn't mean that, Ma'am. We just didn't want you to be embarrassed. Please have a seat. Hank and I want to make your acquaintance."

Doris said, "We feel right at home. You're the first men we every met when we were nude," and they all smiled."

Tex said, "Then you're not married?"

"Well, we aren't now, but aren't you going to make honest women of us?"

Tex and Hank both turned red, and Martha said, "Don't mind my sister's humor. She would see something humorous, if they were about to hang us."

Tex said, "Hank and I were talking and both of us thought you were the two most beautiful women we have ever seen."

Martha looked at Doris and said, "I think we are on the right track, Doris. We have enchanted these two."

Doris said, "We are Doris and Martha Singleton. We hail from around Greeley, Colorado where our father owns a small ranch. He also farms potatoes and feed for our animals."

Tex said, "I'm Wilber Horton and this is Henry Vaughn. However, everyone calls us Tex and Hank. We both hail from South Texas, but found a job here in Wyoming on the Beasley Ranch. It's a large ranch and the owner is from England. Hank and I tend a section up here and live in this line shack in the winter."

Hank said, "We believe in divine intervention. Last night after supper, Tex suggested that we go down to the river and watch it awhile. We never did that before. We believe God sent us there. We both threw our ropes further than we ever tried to rope a steer and the loops went over you like God had placed them there, and we pulled in two angles sent directly from heaven."

Doris looked at Martha and said, "I don't know about you, but I'm in love."

Both men turned red and Martha said, "Two unused men. I believe they're right. It must have been divine intervention."

Tex looking serious, said, "You may be kidding, but I'm not. I feel God sent you here. I must admit that we are just two dumb cowboys that just finished the third grade. We know nothing, but poking cows. As far as being unused, we have both known saloon girls. We just want you to know all about us."

Doris said, "These are the two most honest men in the world, Martha. Daddy would just love them. I want to take them home."

Tex said are you just funning us, Ma'am, because Hank and I are dead serious. We would both marry you today if we had anyway of supporting you. However, Hank just said, 'We're just two dumb cowboys who make thirty a month and found.'"

Doris said, "Don't worry about your income. If you come with us, you will be working daddies ranch. He has enough land to run a big herd of cattle, but he doesn't because he doesn't want to hire men to do it.

"We do have a Mexican family who farms the feed and potatoes. Daddy gives Roberto half of everything he farms, and he makes a pretty good living. He also furnishes him a house and his wife and daughter helps us at our place."

Doris said, "If you want, you could ranch at our place and see if you like us and the life there."

"You would take us knowing we are just two dumb cowboys?"

"It's divine intervention isn't it?" Martha asked.

"She's right, Hank. We accept your offer. Hank and I have two hundred and eighty dollars saved in our bank account. We have always kept our money together as we are pards."

"Well, the only change there will be, is that your wives will be keeping up with your money now. Have you figured out which one you want?"

"We have, if you agree. Tex likes you Doris and I want you Martha."

"Sounds good to us. We thought the same way. See, divine intervention."

They snow kept coming and came up to the door latch. The men tended to their horses and even rode out to make sure the herd was where they wintered. They had much hay there for them.

While the men were gone. Doris said, "I believe it was divine intervention, Martha. They are perfect. I was beginning to think we would be old maids. How old do you think they are. We are both past twenty-five. I have no idea how old they are. I would guess about our age, but who cares. They love us and have never even kissed us."

"I really believe it was God who brought us together. I think they are the best two men on this earth and God gave them to us. We love the ranch and they know how to run it. It comes at a time when Dad has even mentioned hiring someone. I think he will be pleased as punch."

Martha said, "I don't think we should sleep with them until we are married."

"I don't think they would sleep with us before marriage if we tried to get them to," and they both laughed.

They were snowed in for four days. During that time, they played cards, sang songs and the girls cooked for them. Both men didn't know how to bake pies, but the girls rigged a Dutch oven and made them a couple of apple pies from a barrel of apples the men had."

They were all deliriously happy. After the snow melted, the men rode them to the ranch headquarters at the Beasley ranch. Tex introduced Doris and Martha to Mr. Beasley and explained that they were engaged to be married. He further went on to explain that the cattle were in good shape in their winter place and there was enough hay to last the winter."

Tex then said, "We have to leave now, Mr. Beasley as we are needed on the girl's ranch."

Beasley said, "I can see you have cornered some beautiful women." He then turned to the women and said, "You've got two of the finest men I have ever employed. You may have to cut off some of the bark and rough edges, but I can assure you, you have made the right choice. I give you my blessing and hope you have a long and fruitful life. Let me go get you your wages."

He came back and handed them each two hundred dollars. He said, "Part of that is a wedding present. I want to keep in touch with you, so write me a letter when you get time."

They left for a small town that the railroad went through. They were able to take their horses. They went to Cheyenne and then bought tickets for the girls on a stage and the men followed on their horses. The ranch was only a mile out of Greeley and they made the trip in less than a half hour.

Ed Singleton wanted to know why they were back so soon. After all were in the living room of the house, the girls told the extraordinary story.

At the end Ed said, "I want to pray and thank God for his mercy. They all bowed their heads and Ed prayed. Both Tex and Hank knew they were in the right place.

Ed told the men that he would buy them two hundred heifers in the spring and they could get started.

CHAPTER 14

CALIFORNIA

Alvin's trip to San Francisco was relaxing. He thought of Acula, Holley and Cara. They were all so different, but they all loved him. He began to see how lucky he had been to have known and loved them. He wondered if he would ever get close to Cara. She was a lovely person, but did he love her? He barely knew her, but here he was stuck with her. He liked to be around her, and she was interesting to talk with. It was certainly better than being alone. He had no idea what he would do in life. The Lord had blessed him with all the material wealth he would ever need.

He arrived in San Francisco and went to the best hotel available. The next day he went to the bank to see if the money transfer had been completed. The bank president, a man named Bob Melton, was elated to meet him, as the transfer of money had gone through without a hitch. He invited Alvin to lunch and took him to Fisherman's Wharf to a seafood restaurant.

Bob said, "Mr. Scott I would like to help you invest, as I am a financial consultant as well as the president of my bank. I get great pleasure when I make money for my clients. I charge only ten percent of what I earn you, so our goals are the same."

Alvin said, "Please call me, Alvin, because I'm sure we will be working together. I'll be frank with you, Mr. Melton, I am extremely wealthy. You only received a small portion of my wealth. I'm not bragging, because every cent I have, the Lord gave to me. In my book, he owns it all, I am merely the custodian of it. However, I do want to take good care of his money. I want to give a lot of it away doing his work. Will you help me?"

"There is no pleasure on earth or as fulfilling as giving money to worthy causes. We have an orphanage here, that is just getting by on a shoe string. You will really help those children have a chance in life. We also have some civil war veterans who need help. A woman's organization has taken that on, and I have helped. None of us supported either side during the war, but we now see how it has hurt so many who were engaged in that terrible ordeal. Greta Morris told me that these men were hurt more mentally, than they were physically. They saw horrible things, that no human should have seen. We have two doctors who have recently arrived in our city. Their expertise is healing the mind. They took on the Civil War veterans pro bono."

Alvin said, "I will leave it to you how much and how often you donate to them from my money. I have been thinking about going to Alaska and seeing everything from here to there. My first wife loved nature. We crossed the Rocky Mountains with just backpacks. It was a wonderful experience. However, it got her killed. Indians attacked us, and killed her. I was very fortunate to escape, as I was standing right beside her.

"That has not discouraged me from seeing more wild country, though. On the contrary, I think of her when I am viewing those things, as it reminds me of her loving face. I could never find a woman who adored me like she did. It caused me to adore her."

"Alvin, I have a friend who is a naturalist. He has been to all those places you are talking about. You need to talk to him before you strike out. He may help you plan your trip. His name is Edger Nance."

Alvin met Edger. They talked for sometime about Alvin's trip. In the end Edger said, "You have excited me to where I want to go with you."

"Come along. There is just one thing, I may be bringing a woman. I say maybe, because I met her a few weeks ago. We were in a train wreck on the other side of Ogden, Utah and nearly lost our lives. To my knowledge, we were the only survivors."

"I read about that wreck. They never mentioned your name, but they did say a couple survived along with two women. They gave their names as Doris and Martha Singleton, but they had forgotten yours."

"I asked them not to use our names as the lady was married and I spent a few nights with her in the wilds. Even though nothing happened, her husband my take offense."

"The two ladies lauded you in the news article, saying they would have never survived without you. They wished they could remember your name as they wanted to thank you. I believe the article said they were from Greeley, Colorado."

Alvin was surprised and pleased that Doris and Martha had made it. They were both young and had lives to live.

Ten days later, Alvin answered a knock at his door and there stood Cara. She just came into his arms and kissed him passionately.

Alvin said, "I was sure you would change your mind when you saw your husband again."

"No, I saw what your wives saw in you. You always think of your woman before yourself. You make a woman want you as you listen to her and are interesting to talk with. It's the way you look at me as if you are looking inside me. It only took a few minutes in the dining car to see I wanted you. I want you forever."

"Well, I've planned out our trip. A man who has been to Alaska several times, wants to go with us. He is a naturalist. He taught in a college back East, but gave it up to see the wilds first hand, after his father left him a substantial legacy. Do you mind having him along?"

"No, as long as I have you at night."

"That sounds very intimate. Maybe we should marry first."

"Who knows that besides us."

"A bigamist. I never thought I would be that."

"If you want. I think it would be just as right, being your mistress and it will be less complicated. I'm sure Gerald will divorce me. He can't stand being alone. He needs someone to give orders to and run their life. He was very demanding."

"Let me think about this awhile. Maybe we should get some counseling before we cohabitate. I'm not a prude, but I also believe in God and his commandments."

"I suppose you're right. I've let my lust overwhelm me, I see. I love you so much I want to give you all my love. When you held me at night on our trip, I would have seduced you if we didn't need to have our clothes on."

"That may be why we were in that weather."

"No, I think we were put together by divine province. I knew my first marriage was not sanctioned by God. I should have never married him. I think my father's wealth had diminished to the point that he needed me to marry Gerald. He bailed my father out of a terrible financially scrape and now he's okay. I see we just capitalized on Wanda's death. Gerald saw me only through lust. He was a lustful man and I had heard stories about his indiscretions, but thought I could cure him of that.

"However, before I left Philadelphia, I learned that one of his secretaries had his baby. That was one of the reasons he took the post in Carson City."

"Well, that's in the past now, as even if I don't bed you right away, we will be together."

"Yes, but in torture."

"I'll see what I can do. Give me a little time. I will rent the room next to me and we can be companions until that is worked out."

"How are you going to pay for that? These rooms are expensive."

"I have enough money, don't ever worry about money when you are with me."

"Is your name Vanderbilt instead of Scott?"

"No, but he works for me," and they both laughed.

Alvin talked to Bob Melton and told him he needed to have a good lawyer to help him, should he need one. Bob put him onto Ivan Shulanski. Bob said, "He is not only the best lawyer around, but is very loyal to his clients."

Alvin set an appointment with Ivan and told him the entire story. Ivan said, "You just left the most liberal state for divorces. That is Nevada. Here in California it is very hard to obtain a divorce. If you want, I will try to obtain a divorce for you. I have a colleague in Carson City. He will know Gerald Wilson. I would imagine that Wilson has already sought a divorce. Check with me next week. Thanks for the retainer. I have never had a client who gave me a five-hundred dollar retainer. I will always have your back, Mr. Scott."

"Call me Alvin, Mr. Shulanski. I hope we will become good friends as well as business associates."

"I'm sure we will, as Bob Melton is one of my closest friends."

That night Alvin took Cara to a dinner that had a floorshow. It was a delightful evening. When he kissed her goodnight, she said, "Does it bother you that I would have been your mistress rather than marry you."

"No, it showed that you love me. I love you also, but I cannot do that. I will tell you about a skeleton that is in my closet after we are married a few years. It is one of the reasons I am now a Christian."

"You have whetted my mind, now. I will be forever thinking what you might have done. I will probably laugh when you tell me that you looked with lust at a beautiful woman, once." Alvin turned the key in her door and they parted.

Alvin had asked Edger to plan their trips. He had looked into passenger ships that would take them to Vancouver Island. He wanted to show them a hotel that was in Victoria. He then would look into going to Sitka. Alaska had been purchased by the United States from Russia in 1867. However, many Russians still lived there. Most of which were very happy to get from under the thumb of the Russians. The people who stayed were naturalized as U. S. citizens.

A week after seeing Ivan Shulanski, Alvin got a message from him. Alvin went immediately.

Ivan said, "The day after Cara left Wilson, he filed for divorce. The fifteenth of this month, she will be a free woman."

"Thanks, Ivan, I will be marrying her the sixteenth, and you and your wife are invited. It will give me time to plan the marriage, so it will please, Cara.

"Would you do me a favor? I would like to contact Doris and Martha Singleton. They were headed to see an aunt of theirs here in San Francisco. They could come to the wedding and see their aunt on the same trip."

"I'll get that done for you, Alvin."

A wedding invitation was sent to the Singleton ranch. Both girls were elated to get the invitation. They talked their new husbands into going with them.

They arrived a day before the wedding. Alvin had already reserved them rooms at the same hotel that he and Cara were staying.

The girls told them their story. Cara had both women in the wedding and their husbands were ushers. The wedding was a gala affair, after which the girls and their husbands departed for Greeley.

CHAPTER 15

THE ALASKAN TRIP

Before they left, Edgar made sure they had taken everything that would make the trip easier and more fun. They brought rods and reels, rifles, handguns and two shotguns. He made sure they had good eider sleeping bags, canteens and mosquito repellant. They brought netting for night time and hats with netting to cover their faces and necks. They also brought a case of brandy.

Edgar said, "They don't have good liquor in Alaska. There's a shortage of women, but you brought a supply for that too," and they both laughed.

They then sailed on a ship that accommodated passengers as well as freight. The ship they were on, was taking them to Vancouver Island. Edgar wanted to show them a hotel in Victoria. It was unique and luxurious. They spent three days there as they had three different floorshows at night. They spent the day with a guide showing them historical sights. They were also waiting on a ship bound for Anchorage, Alaska that would stop at Sitka.

After Sitka, they went straight to Anchorage. Edgar had planned a trip from there to Fairbanks where they would hopefully sail down the Yukon river. They bought three horses in Anchorage at a hundred and twenty dollars each and eighty for a mule. It was twice what they would pay in Seattle. However, Edgar had told them that prices would be at least double what they were in San Francisco. They packed a tent, their bedrolls and cooking gear onto the mule, and were off on a bright, sun shinny day.

Edgar had been on this trail before, so there was little worry. In fact everyone was in great spirits, when they left on their trip. In Fairbanks they planned to sell their animals and find someone who would take them in a boat down the Yukon River.

Edgar had never taken that trip, but he had heard a lot of stories about it. He looked forward to experiencing, the well over thousand mile journey, down the Yukon. Cara was somewhat apprehensive, but if Alvin wanted to go, then she wanted to go.

The trip to Fairbanks took them well over a week, and they were all worn out when they arrived. They found a hotel and decided to stay there a couple of days.

They found a man named Oscar Bright, who would take them in a fair sized boat to Galena. The boat was a twenty-five foot Boston whaler. He was hauling supplies to Galena, but had room for the three and their trappings. That trip was over six hundred miles, but Oscar assured them there were numerous places to stop. This was true to a point, but he failed to tell them most of the places were with natives who lived in places that it was better to campout than be indoors.

The trip began alright. The third day they stopped at a minors camp. There were four men, who were pretty rough. Oscar got along with them, but one particular man was a large, obnoxious minor, named Baxter. He took a fancy to Cara and kept making lewd remarks to her. She told him that she was married, but this didn't phase him at all. That is when Alvin stepped in.

Alvin said, "If you persist in annoying my wife, I will have to shoot you."

This got Baxter's attention, but he merely pulled his knife and came at Alvin who pulled his gun and shot him in the leg. He fell to the ground grasping his leg and yelled to the others, "Kill him!" Two of the minors came to Baxter's aid. The other said, "You will have to pay for this. Baxter will be laid up for weeks and it will slow our operation."

Alvin said, "I don't want to kill the lot of you, but if I have to, I will. I suggest you take Baxter and move back to your diggings."

"Or you'll what," said one of the minors.

"Or I'll kill the lot of you. Just say the word and this will become a shooting war."

Cara and Edgar were mortified. Oscar had seen these things fester before, and was now planning their next move.

Another minor, named Mort, said, "You think this is over? Well it's not."

"It's over unless you want to have more of your party injured or possibly dead. I was in the army and I'm accustomed to war. Just say the word and it can start here."

The other two hadn't said anything. They just picked Baxter up and took him away. The other minor stared at

Alvin a moment or so, absorbing what he had said, then turned and followed the others.

Oscar said, "It will be dangerous traveling at night, but I suggest we leave here at once. It will take us all being very alert, but the moon is bright and we can see most of the obstructions if everyone is alert."

They all began packing and fifteen minutes later they were traveling down the Yukon. Cara spoke first and said, "You were magnificent, Alvin."

Oscar said, "That may be, but we may have not seen the last of them. Some of these men are vindictive and will carry a grudge until they feel it is satisfied."

"Well, someone will have to stay with Baxter, so there will be just two of them. Besides, it would interrupt their mining."

"That may be, but I've seen these type of men. We had better be on the lookout for them. They will want to kill us and misuse Cara."

"I suggest we don't camp with these type of men in the future, Oscar."

"I made a mistake. I didn't figure that man's passion for women. They have no morals and take what they want unless they see it will injure them if they do. Let's just hope they weigh the value of revenge against something they may lose, if they try to pursue us."

They were fortunate that the moon was bright. The Yukon is notorious for rocks protruding near or just under the surface. This and other things can rip a boat apart. Oscar knew another spot and was hoping they could reach it soon. He found the spot and an hour later they were all asleep. The sun woke them up. After a quick breakfast, they packed and were gone again.

Back at the mining camp they tried, but could not stop the bleeding of Baxter's leg. They finally cauterized it, but the shock put Baxter in cardiac arrest and he died that night.

The men were upset. The leader, Mort Hagar said, "That guy can't go unpunished. Baxter would want his heart cut out."

Leo said, "Let's go after him after we bury Baxter in the morning."

The other man, Tim Easter, said, "I wasn't that fond of Baxter in the first place. He brought it on himself. I, for one, will not pursue those people. It may get us all killed and for what, a mean bastard that anyone would have shot if they insulted his wife like he did."

Leo said, "He's got a point, Mort. He really deserved getting shot. Most men would have just killed him. This guy just shot him in the leg. We lost him, as we aren't that skilled in doctoring."

Mort said, "You do what you want, but I'm taking one of the canoes and going after them."

"Are you going after revenge or the woman?" Leo asked.

"Mort grinned and said, "Both."

"There are three of them. One of them will surely kill you," Leo said.

"Well, I haven't had a woman in so long, I'll chance it. I would sure like one of you to go along."

Neither of them answered, so Mort began packing his things. He was gone an hour later. Being several hours behind them, he felt he could catch them because his canoe was much faster.

He was right. Just after lunch he spotted them. They were just a dot on the river, but Mort had very good eyes.

He paddled to shore, as he didn't want them to know he was pursuing them. He waited just a few minutes, then paddled out keeping to the edge of the river as much as possible.

Oscar didn't stop for lunch. He told Edgar to just feed them out of his knapsack. He had some jerky there. They were all worn out when it started turning dark. Clouds were gathering and they all knew they were in for a rain.

Oscar guided them to shore at a place that was close to trees. They pulled the boat up onto a sandy beach, and Oscar used a chain to secure the boat to a tree, as he knew the river may rise.

While he was doing that Edgar and Cara were gathering firewood and Alvin was looking for shelter. He found it on the lee side of a bluff. It was an overhang that would shield them from the wind and the coming rain.

Alvin then started a fire as Cara and Edgar came with armloads of firewood. Oscar came dragging a dead tree. They all went into the trees and by nightfall had enough wood to last the night. They had supper and then all turned in so they could get an early start.

Meanwhile, Mort had spotted the smoke from their fire. He found a place near to them and beached his canoe. He scouted the area and found their boat. It had begun to rain and it came down in torrents.

Mort used this as a shield and made his way to their boat. He removed the chain and pushed the boat out into the channel. The water took it and he watched it disappear into the night.

He then returned to his canoe and removed his trappings and then carried his canoe up a bank and hid it under a deadfall. He also used this as a shelter. He went to sleep then.

The rain had ended by morning and they cooked a good breakfast. Oscar said, "Make something for lunch as we will travel all day today without stopping. We need to get far down the river, just encase."

They packed and carried their gear down to where their boat had been. Oscar at once checked the chain. He said, "The boat couldn't have gotten loose on its own. Someone undid the chain and either swiped the boat or just let it drift down stream. If someone stole the boat, it was probably natives, but if it were just turned loose, it was those miners. We need to find a place to defend ourselves, because if it is those miners, they are out to kill us."

Alvin said, "It can't be over two of them, because they would not leave Baxter alone. I suggest that we arm ourselves and search for them. If one of us comes upon them, shoot twice in the air. We will then know where they are.

"I'm not trying to scare anyone, but this will be a fight to the death. When you shoot, shoot to kill. That is the only way we will get out of this. I know the boat was let loose by the miners."

Oscar said, "I think Alvin is right. It's the miners. I also agree that we need to bring the fight to them. I will go upstream and Edgar, you go downstream."

Edgar said, "I'm no warrior. I can shoot a gun, but I'm not much good at that. If I ran onto the miners, they would kill me easily."

Alvin said, "I will go downstream. You return to our camp. We will help you bring the gear before we start out. We can then build a place there to hold them off. I think you would be safe there, as with that bluff, they can't come for you unless they expose themselves, and they aren't about to do that. Besides either Oscar or I will run into them first as they can't get to our fort unless going through us."

Cara said, "I want to go with you, Alvin."

"No, Cara, I need to move very quietly. I don't want to be worrying about you. This is going to be tricky."

Cara didn't argue as she knew Alvin was right. They were now at their shelter. They dragged some deadfalls to the camp and constructed a makeshift fort.

Edgar said, "I feel that Cara and I will be safe now. Can you shoot, Cara?"

"I can, Edger, and will, as our lives are at stake."

Alvin and Oscar took their rifles and a box of extra shells. They also crammed their pockets full of jerky and brought a canteen and left.

Mort had figured they would have to come after him. He found a good spot in the crag of the bluff. He took his canteen and enough food to last him a day. He figured that he would just wait them out. Sooner or later they would have to move.

He was right. About mid morning he saw movement and then Oscar came into view. He waited until he had an easy shot then shot him. The bullet went through Oscar's body and killed him instantly.

Mort waited for five or ten minutes and there was no moment so he climbed down and turned Oscar's body over with his foot. He could tell he was dead, but still felt his neck and there was no pulse. He then picked him up and carried him to the river. He emptied his pockets and took off his coat and boots. He then set him adrift in the river. The river was moving at a good pace and took the body downstream.

Mort watched the body go further out without sinking and down the river. He then picked up everything he had taken from Oscar and decided to wait at his place in the crag and see if anyone came to check on the shot he had fired.

Alvin heard the shot as did Edgar and Cara. Edgar said, "We will stay put. That shot was from Oscar, but we will let Alvin and Oscar handle it. They are both quite capable."

Alvin heard the shot and moved quickly back. He was walking near shore when he saw Oscars body floating by some fifty feet out in the river. He then knew he must be very careful.

He moved very carefully not leaving anything to chance. He knew about how far Oscar had gone as he knew how far he had come. He wouldn't have to be too careful until he came to where they had parted. From there he moved very carefully.

As he moved he could see Oscar's trail. He moved very slowly now, using trees as shelter. He finally came to a point where he spotted fresh blood and knew the miners were near. He decided to hunker down and wait for the miners to make a move. He stayed that way until dark and there was no movement. After dark, the same moon was still bright. He carefully made his way back to their campsite. When he was fifty feet away he called, "Cara, I'm coming in, don't shoot me."

Cara wrapped her arms about him when he was within their fort. Edgar had a small fire going and Cara had made a stew. He was really hungry as he had not eaten since morning.

When they were having coffee, Alvin said, "Oscar is dead. I saw his body float by on the river. I reached the place where he was killed, and waited all afternoon, but no one moved. I felt they were out there, but was probably waiting for me to make a move.

"Tomorrow early, I will make a place for me between the fort and the beach. While I was with Cuela, I learned a valuable lesson, and that is patients. He who wait's the longest, generally is the one who stays alive. In this case, I am willing to wait a week if need be."

Edgar said, "That sounds wise to me."

Alvin slept only about five hours, then left camp with a supply of food and a full canteen. It took him three hours to find the place he wanted. He then sat and waited.

Meanwhile, Mort had figured what Alvin would do. He had also surmised that Edgar was not a warrior and was probably staying with the woman while Alvin was stalking him. He decided to wait two days before he did anything. They would then wonder if he had left.

He decided that they would move downstream looking for a village or other people to help them. Mort waited until night, then carried his canoe to the river. He packed his gear into the canoe and went out onto the river. He traveled about two miles, then made his way to shore. He found a good place to ambush them. He hid his canoe again and waited.

Two days passed and when Alvin came in that night he said, "They may have left after they killed Oscar thinking the score was even. I say we wait another two days and then walk downstream and look for help."

"We will have to," Edgar said, "Our supplies are about gone. We will soon have to live off the land."

They waited the two days, then started out. About mid afternoon they reached the place where Mort was. He took careful aim and shot Alvin in the leg. He then shot Edgar through the body. He walked out holding his rifle to his cheek and said, "If either of you move, I will kill you."

Alvin had dropped his rifle when he was shot and it was out of reach. Cara had no weapon, so she just stood there. Mort kicked Alvin's rifle away. It was at a part of the shore that had a steep slope and slid into the water.

Mort then took his toe and turned Edgar's body over. He was dead. He then took a length of rope and dragged Alvin to a tree and tied him up. He laughed and said, "I'm not going to kill you, Alvin. I'll just let mother nature take her time doing that."

He then motioned Cara toward his canoe. He had everything packed, as he wanted everything ready when the time came. He said, "Get in the front of the canoe and pick up a paddle. He then climbed in behind her and they shoved off going up stream. The paddling was strenuous for Cara and she soon tired out. Mort could see she couldn't go on, so he paddled toward shore.

He said, "If you give me any trouble, I'll shoot you in the stomach and you will probably last three or four days before you die. I once heard of an Indian who cut a squaw's stomach open and pulled out her intestines and tied them to a tree."

Cara was very scared as she knew the viciousness of the miner. They rested an hour and then were back onto the water. The going was slow, but Cara did her best.

That night they made camp. He sent her for firewood and told her about the bears of that region. When they had eaten,

Mort said, "Take off all your clothes. I want to see what you look like."

He had pulled out his knife and was grinning at her. She spread her bedroll and disrobed. Mort watched her with a evil grin on his face. He then walked over and took her down and raped her. She put up no fight and it was over shortly.

He put his bedroll on top of hers and tied her ankle to his ankle, so she knew there was no chance of escape. She slept fitfully knowing what she was in for. She tried not to think of Alvin and what he must be going through.

The next morning, Mort raped her again before he fed her breakfast. By noon they were opposite of the mine site. It was about mid afternoon when they walked up to the mine. Both the other miners were out taking a breather and smiled when they saw Cara.

Mort said, "You can take that smile off you faces as you ain't getting her for free. She's my woman and I'm going to charge you five dollars a poke."

"Come on Mort, even the whores in Fairbanks don't charge that much."

"But we ain't in Fairbanks, Leo, and that's the price I'll ask for. I'll just take it out of your part of the gold after we sell it."

Tim said, "You are a hard man, Mort," then pulled his gun and shot Mort through the chest. Mort was so surprised he just stared at Tim and said, "You killed me."

"No, you killed yourself by charging us too much. Mort then fell and Leo felt his pulse, then turned and said, "He's dead. I never liked him or Baxter. I say good riddance."

"Yeah, but now we have to bury him."

Cara was mortified at the cruelness of the men. She knew she was in for a hard time. She began to think of running away, but how could she do that, and where would she go. She began forming a plan in her mind. There were three canoes she knew of. If she would steal one and ruin the others, so they couldn't be repaired, she could go back and find Alvin. She knew she must bide her time and these men would misuse her morning and night, but she would just have to endure it.

She then thought of playing one against the other. They would be here all summer. She would play up to one of them and try to get him to like her or even love her. She had never done any of this.

CHAPTER 16

NASO AND SOLESA

A French trader had set up a trading post on the Yukon River in 1860. He knew that there was going to be a Civil War in America and he thought that many people would try to escape that war by coming to Alaska. As the Yukon River provided most of the travel in Alaska he went there. He found a place about halfway from Fairbanks and Galena and built a trading post. It was in a place that had great exposure to the river. He also knew that there were several tribes that were near there, that he could trade guns, steel implements, such as shovels, picks and other things for animal skins. The skins were in great demand at that time.

There were several tribes north of the Yukon River. They began trading with the Frenchman and it really enhanced their lives. With repeating rifles, they could acquire many more skins and buy the steel implements that the Frenchman had.

Naso belonged to a tribe northwest of the trading post. He had married a woman, Solesa, from a neighboring tribe who didn't get along with their tribe. This caused tension. Solesa was a quiet person and tried to stay away from the other women as they looked down on her. Naso could see this, but said nothing. However, he had it in his mind to move away and start his own tribe.

He found a place that was about ten miles north of the Frenchman's trading post that was just what he wanted. It was at a place that had a hot spring. His tribe and the other tribes thought this an area of bad spirits, and stayed away from it. This notion had been passed down for generations.

Naso thought this a superstition that had no merit. He hunted alone and always went to this area as the others were afraid to go there. This gave him an area where the game was plentiful with no others to compete with.

He had become friendly with the Frenchman, who called himself, Frenchy. Naso had traded with him. He could tell that Frenchy had built a substantial place out of logs. It was more insulated than the yurts that his tribe used and much larger. As Naso's and Solesa's family was growing, Naso decided to build such a place as the Frenchman had. He told Frenchy about the hot spring and Frenchy gave him the idea of piping the hot water a short distance to the place he wanted to build, so that the warm water could warm his house and possibly a barn in the cold winters. Frenchy told his trading partner to bring the pipes necessary and in a year or so Naso had the pipe he needed to do the job. He knew this would save countless hours of gathering wood or peat for fuel.

The Frenchman had seen this done before and helped plan the heating process with Naso. He consulted with Frenchy and even hired a man who knew how to build large log buildings to help him. He suggested to Naso to hire the same man to help built his house. The carpenter was very good at his trade and knew about all the modern facilities that very few people possessed, such as a sink for a cooking area and an indoor toilet that took sewage away to a small canyon near the house. It even had a bathtub and a hand sink as hot water was no problem.

Naso never told Solesa about the house. He wanted it as a surprise. His oldest daughter was now sixteen and he didn't want her to marry any of the local men. As he looked at them, most of these men were just over five feet in statue. He wanted his daughters to have large sons. He had seen the white men, who came occasionally to the trading post and they were all nearly six feet tall or over. He, also, didn't want anyone from his tribe to marry into his family, because of the friction that went on, not only internally, but with other tribes. He despised his own people, because of the way they treated Solesa and his daughters.

He now had four daughters that ranged in age from sixteen down to eleven. He had no boys which he dearly wanted. It had now been eleven years since his wife was last pregnant. Naso had an accident to his groan area and they both thought that must have been the reason for Solesa not being able to become pregnant.

It took over two years for Naso to build his house. It was like the white men's houses Frency had showed him in magazines.

After Naso had the house completed with its heating system from the hot spring, he began building a travois. Solesa asked why he was building it and he said, "We are moving. Pack everything that you want, as we are moving away from the tribe. Solesa was shocked, but pleased. She told the girls and made them promise not to tell anyone.

There was a young man who was thinking of getting married, so Naso was able to sell his yurt to him. The young man said nothing about buying the yurt, because he wanted to show it to her father after he had furnished it like he thought it should be. The girls father would then see him prosperous and give his permission to wed his daughter.

While everyone in the tribe was eating their noon meal, Naso's family loaded the travois and left. No one missed them as no one had anything to do with his family. As they traveled his oldest daughter, said, "I'm glad to be gone. Everyone shunned us. I had no chance of marrying."

Naso said, "I don't want you to marry anyone from our tribe or the other tribes. They are not for us. We need strong sons from you and your sisters if we are to build our own tribe."

"How will we do that, father?"

"I will find a way." His daughter didn't reply as she had great faith in her father. She and her sisters thought their father the smartest man in the world.

They camped the first night. It was summer, so it was easy. At the close of the second day, they came to a hill that overlooked a large log house. They all stopped and Solesa said, "Look, there is a white man's home. Shall we go around it?"

Naso didn't immediately answer. He just let them all look at the log home. The youngest said, "That is the grandest building in the world."

Naso said, "I have seen pictures of bigger buildings, but it is large. It is our new home."

They were all stunned. Solesa said, "You are joking of course?"

"No, it's our new home. I have been building it for five years. You will be amazed when you see it."

The girls all screamed with joy. They then went to the home and investigated it. They were all intensely happy.

There were several rooms. All were amazed as Naso showed them the kitchen and bathroom. He showed them how to use the toilet. There were lamps for every room and two in the large room. Naso lit all of them, so that all the rooms were illuminated. Every time one of the girls passed by Naso they would hug him.

He had bought beds for them all. They had three bedrooms. He and Saleso had one room and there were bunk beds in two of the rooms for the girls. There were other things to show them, but he would do that the next day.

Each year they went to the river to fish. The Frenchman liked Naso and showed him how to use nets to gather fish. This helped greatly in their winter food supply.

One year the trading post burned. It appeared that Frenchy was burned in the building. Naso didn't know of it for a month when he came to trade with the Frenchman. He was filled with sorrow. He decided to clear the area of the burned building and make it look like nothing had been there. He had a plan in mind to build his own trading post someday and didn't want others to see this good place on the river.

The time came that they were to fish for their winter food. Naso had a place that was easy to cast their nets near where the trading post had been. It was only a few yards from the trading post. He had told his family about the fire and they were all sad.

When they were nearly to the trading post area, they heard shots. They stopped and Naso said, "It may be only a hunter, however, keep your guns ready."

He had taught every girl to shoot and they were ready. When they arrived at the area, they saw a man tied to a tree. He had been shot through the leg. Naso quickly untied the man. While he was doing that, Solesa was starting a fire and one of the girls gathered water in a pot to heat. No one said a word, but moved with efficiency.

Soleso knew just what to do. She could see that the bullet had gone straight through his leg. She took the ramming rod from Naso's musket and after holding it in the fire for awhile she put it through the wound to keep it from becoming infected. She then cauterized both sides of the wound. All this time Alvin was unconscious.

One of the girls said, "Will he live?"

Solesa said, "I'm not certain, he's lost a lot of blood and may develop infection or a fever. I would say he has and even chance."

Looking at Alvin's size, Naso said, "We need him for our daughters. We need babies and this man can give us that."

"What if he doesn't want to stay with us?" The oldest daughter, Leah asked.

"No matter, we will have the babies. He is a white man and they are much bigger than our kind.

Solesa said, "As you are unable to make me pregnant, I may be able to get pregnant by him, also. What do you think?"

"I think it a good idea. I would like a big son. I will be getting on in years and if we can have sons that will help us, it will be good. The daughters now ranged from fifteen to twenty years of age.

They had brought the hides to make a shelter for them and began cutting poles to make a framework, then stretch the hides. By evening they had a fine yurt as large as the one they lived in while living with the tribe. Alvin had not wakened As they were eating that evening, Solesa explained the plan to her daughters. They all smiled and were eager. Naso explained the advantages of having a white man father their first born.

He said, "We may find you husbands with another tribe. They will not know that these children are yours. The family needs these babies if we are to survive. I am getting on in age and in another twenty years, I may not be able to do what I do now." They all nodded thinking their father a wise man.

They now had Alvin in their shelter and the mother slept with him to keep him warm.

The next morning, Alvin woke. He knew someone was sleeping with him as he could feel the body heat. When he stirred the person with him rose and he could tell it was a woman. His leg hurt terribly and he groaned. The woman went outside to relieve herself, then returned.

Everyone was now up and a fire was brought back to life. The woman knew Alvin would need to relieve himself, so she asked the older daughter to help her with him. They each got under Alvin's arms and took him outside. He was in excruciating pain, but he made it outside. The mother began opening his pants, but Alvin moved her arm away and did it himself. He motioned them away as he stood on his good leg and went.

They then took him back into shelter and laid him down. One of the daughters had cooked some broth and brought it to him. The mother helped him by spoon feeding him.

Alvin was very thirsty, but the mother only gave him a sip at a time. He drank all the broth and the mother could see he was thirsty and gave him some more water.

She could tell Alvin was in terrible pain, so she used a medicine they had for extreme pain. She put it in the water he drank. In a few minutes Alvin began to feel light headed, but the pain was gone. He was not quite awake, but not asleep either. It was a dream world that had people he didn't know coming and going. He liked the dream and he had no pain.

By this time the father and all the children were placing the nets, while the mother tended to Alvin. She had stripped him from the waist down and with her hand brought him to an erection, then mounted him. He felt he was with Cuela making love to her. It was a wonderful feeling.

By noon the medicine began to wear off and the pain returned. It was terrible pain. He was able to eat some, but he had little appetite due to the pain.

The next day, the mother told the older daughter what to do and they gave him more medicine. As the family worked on their fishing the older daughter was making love to Alvin.

Each day the medicine would be given to Alvin and another daughter would mount him.

After a week Alvin had done all the girls. He was much better, although he was still weak and had some pain. He had also grown fond of the medicine and asked the mother for more. She gave him a smaller dose each day until he was weaned off the medicine.

Even though Alvin wanted the medicine, Solesa said, "No, it is for extreme pain, and you are not in extreme pain.

Each girl took their turn sleeping with Alvin, but he made no move toward them. One of them even tried to entice him by caressing his genitals, but Alvin turned away.

They now had enough fish and they packed up and left. Alvin could walk with a crutch, but he tired very easily. One of the girls stayed back with him, while the others went on to their permanent home, which was nearly ten miles away. It took Alvin two days to cover that amount of ground. However, one of the girls was always with him and made him a bed at night.

Three weeks later, Alvin developed a fever and was sick for a week. They all thought he would die, but he pulled through. After two months Alvin was getting around fairly well. He had decided to stay another month to be sure he was able to travel. He knew he was closer to Fairbanks than Galena.

He had integrated with the family and liked all of them.

It was now turning cold and Alvin knew he should not travel in the winter time. He had now picked up enough of the language to communicate with them. They had a very different culture and they talked about the differences. He liked them, but knew he should go back and find out about Cara.

It had been nearly four months since he had been shot. Solesa and all the girls except one, were now pregnant, but Alvin had no clue they were. Unbeknown to Alvin, they gave him the medicine in his water. That night he slept with the one who wasn't pregnant. He again had the erotic dream of making love to Cuela. He had no idea that he had made love to the daughter.

As spring approached Alvin asked Naso to take him to the river. He said, "I may be able to wave down a boat to take me up or downstream. I must get back, I have a wife to see about."

Naso took him. Before he left, Alvin hugged all the women and all rubbed their noses to his nose. They were all very happy with what he had given them.

When they reached the river Alvin told the father he did not need to stay. If he found no boats in a few days, he would return to them. The father turned to go and Alvin handed him a twenty dollar gold piece. The father had left him with a three day supply of food.

He now had a bed that had fir branches stacked up, so he would sleep easier. He had built a table out of a rock that had a flat rock on top of it. He had another rock as a seat.

His leg had improved to the point that he never thought about it anymore.

While he was waiting, he went over the shooting that had occurred here. He remembered that his rifle had been kicked into the river. There was a pool there and he wondered if the rifle was still there. The river was clear at this point and he saw it. He used the rope that was used to tie him up and was able to fish out the rifle. It had corroded some, but he believed he could salvage it. He dismantled it and cleaned every inch of it. He had some bear grease and used it to oil and clean the barrel. He shot it and it worked fine.

It had been four days since he had been there. He was packing up to go back, when he saw a tugboat going downstream. He shot three times in the air and came to the bank and waved.

The tug changed coarse and came to the bank. By this time Alvin had all his gear tied up in a skin that Naso had left him. The tug was able to get close to the bank. Alvin threw his pack aboard and jumped to the deck and the tug backed out and continued their trip.

Alvin said, "Are you headed to Galena?"

"Yes. How did you get stranded?"

"My boat pulled away during a rainstorm."

"It happens," the boatman said.

They tied up at night, and in a couple of nights they came to Galena. Alvin handed the boatman a five dollar gold piece and left the boat. In Galena he found a doctor to look at his leg. The doctor said, "It seems to have healed pretty good on its own. Whoever, cauterized this wound did an excellent job."

He went to a general store and bought a nice change of clothes. He then went to a barbershop and had a shave and a haircut. After that he got a hotel room and had a hot bath and changed into his new clothes. He felt somewhat guilty knowing what Cara was going through.

***

Meanwhile, Cara had worked her charms on Leo She knew Tim was too violent, but thought she may be able to make Leo fall in love with her.

The first thing she told Leo was that she liked him, but didn't like to make love in front of Tim. Leo complied and they went off to make love.

Tim could see that Leo was getting sweet on Cara, so just to humiliate him, he said, "Cara, I want you to use your mouth on me. You can watch Leo."

Tim had sat down in a chair and lowered his pants exposing himself. He said, "Come on over Cara."

Cara looked at Leo and said, "If you love me you will stop this."

Leo by this time was in love with Cara. He drew his gun and said, "If you want to live any longer, you will never speak to Cara again like that."

"Oh, so Leo has fallen in love. If you marry her just remember how many times all of us had her, and how many ways we have had her. She's not that bad, but I've had better whores. Are you going to show her off to your kin, Leo."

As Tim was talking he had worked his gun into his hands. As Leo was about to speak, Tim drew his gun and shot Leo through the head. He was dead before he hit the ground. Tim said, "Now, you can come on over and give me what I want."

Cara was amazed at how calloused Tim was. She then went over and gave him what he wanted, as she knew not to do so, could spell her death.

As Tim was pulling up his pants he said, "Now that you have made me kill Leo, you have to take his place in the mine. He wasn't much there either."

They buried Leo in a shallow grave.

Cara worked hard each day. After work they went to a spring and washed up. Tim always made Cara bathe him, after which he did her. She was now getting use to being misused and thought, *This must be how a whore feels. It is just like another task to do. I guess I will become a whore if I get out of this mess."*

Tim was getting careless as he thought Cara had resigned herself to his way.

One night when he was doing her she worked her hand over his pistol pulled it and shot him in the chest. He was amazed. He said, "What have you done?"

"I just killed you." She stood and as he was naked and on his back she shot his genitals off. He screamed in pain. Cara said, "Just in case you live, you won't have much to live for now."

She then turned and put her clothes on, then came back. She said, "How does it feel now that you are a woman?"

He just glared at her then his eyes became fixed and she knew he was dead. She thought about burying him, but then thought, *"Let the wolves and buzzards eat him."* She then went through his clothes and took what money he had. She knew he had more, but he must have had it hidden.

She gathered up what she thought she would need, most of it food and a bedroll, and went to the river camp to spend the night. She spent three days there before she saw a tugboat going upstream. She hailed the boat by shooting into the air. The tug picked her up and took her to Fairbanks.

She had very little money, so she fixed herself up the best she could and asked where the best saloon was in Fairbanks. The man she was asking looked her up and down and said, "Are you looking for a job as a sporting woman."

"Not if I can find something else, but I lost all my money in a boating accident on the river and now have to seek employment anywhere I can get it."

"I own an exclusive sporting house. We only cater to the genteel. If you would like, I will employ you. I will give you a quarter of what you earn."

"I'll consider it, if it's half."

"No one will pay that."

"They will if they have me in their employment."

"He looked at her again and said, "I'll do it, if I get privileges once a week."

She looked at him and said, "Done."

She liked her new surroundings. The place was nice and the food was good. Her room was furnished like she had pictured rooms like this to be. As she laid down that night, she thought, *"I guess Gerald was right. He said I would become a whore and here I am. I would have never thought it. When I have enough money I will go downstream and bury Alvin. What a shame. I really loved him. He would be disappointed to know I am now a whore. Those miners gave me some pretty good training. I think they did me everyway a person could think of. I hate to admit it, but I began to enjoy some of it."*

CHAPTER 17

GOING HOME

Alvin hired five men and told them he would pay each fifty dollars for a weeks work. He said, "Four miners took my wife at a mining camp up river. She is a prisoner and I want to rescue her. These men killed two of my colleagues in cold blood, so you see this will be very dangerous. It shouldn't take over a week."

He hired the tug for a week's work and they left. It was now over seven month since he had been shot. They arrived at the miner's campsite. They went ashore and spread out. They arrived at the mine and saw three graves and a man that the varmints had ravaged. Just a skeleton with very little meat on it. They exhumed the bodies and all were male. He then had no idea what had happened to Cara.

They buried the remaining body and went back to the river camp. Alvin found their canoes. He knew if Cara were still alive she would have taken one of the canoes down river to Galena, so he assumed that they had killed her and didn't want anyone to find her body.

Alvin went back to Galena and spent a lot of time examining his life. Everyone he knew ended up dead. He warned Cara. She must have died a terrible death at the hands of those miners.

He decided to go back to San Francisco. Edgar had a sister there who he needed to tell. He decided to tell her that it was just an accident, not to shift the blame from himself, but he thought it would be easier, if she thought it were an accident.

He found a tugboat going to Fairbanks, and got passage on it. He arrived in Fairbanks and went to a hotel there. All the hotels were austere. He had a room about eight feet wide and ten feet long with a bed that was hard and lumpy. He went downstairs to have a drink. A man was standing in the lobby and he saw the disgusted look on Alvin's face. He walked up to Alvin and said, "Would you like to go to an elegant bar that serves excellent brandy?"

Alvin turned to him with a smile and said, "Are you just teasing me?"

"No, I know of such a place, but I must warn you that the brandy there is expensive, but the atmosphere is such that it is worth the higher cost."

Alvin said, "Let's go."

They left and went into a very nice place. There were many very nice looking women and Alvin knew at once it was a bawdy house. However, he knew he could just drink and enjoy the scenery. He looked at the man with him and said, "I insist on buying you a couple drinks." "No use to insist, I will accept willingly," and they both laughed.

The man had many funny stories to tell Alvin and for the first time since the shooting, he was happy again.

This was the place that Cara worked. She had just come down the stairs with a client when she saw Alvin. She immediately turned around and went back up the stairs. The place was built where a railing went around the second floor and one could look down on the first floor.

Cara found a chair that she pulled to a place where she had a view of Alvin and his friend. Several girls approached the two. After about a half hour of drinking the man with Alvin went with a girl.

A girl who Cara had befriended came out of a room with a man and she stopped and asked, "Why are you sitting up here, Cara?"

"My ex-husband is down there at the bar. I surely don't want him to know that I'm a whore, now."

"I know what you mean. He's cute, do you mind me approaching him?"

"No, but I can tell you right now you're wasting your time. However, I would like you to talk to him and find out what he has been up to. I will give you a dollars to dig all the information you can from him. Ask him if he has been married. If he says yes, ask him to tell you what happened to his last wife. He's a very generous person and will buy you several drinks. He is also rich."

Cara's friend was named Cheryl. She said, "I'll bet you that dollar you will pay me, that I can get him up to my room for a little sport."

"You've got yourself a bet, Cheryl."

In just a minute Cheryl was sitting by Alvin. Cheryl said, "Do you mind if I sit by you?"

"Why no, I would like the company of a beautiful woman."

"My, you are nice."

Alvin pointed at the bar tender and pointed to Cheryl. The bar tender came down with a glass and poured Cheryl a drink."

Cheryl said, "You are a gentleman. Are you married?"

"No, I'm a widower. I lost my wife several months ago."

"My that is terrible. Would you tell me about it?"

"She was killed by some miners. All of them are dead now. We couldn't figure out how they all died. They shot me in the leg between here and Galena. They took her and must have killed her. They hid her body so no one would know what they did."

"That is a terrible story. I'm so sorry for you. I am so moved I want to do something for you. Could I comfort you tonight. I feel I can help you. Would you let me try?"

"No, no one can help me. I caused her death. I have been married three times and everyone of them died a terrible death. Each one was more terrible than the other. I will never get close to a woman again as I am jinxed. Every woman who loves me will die and I cannot do that to another woman no matter what."

"I don't believe in jinxes. They were merely coincidences."

"You may think that now, but if you came with me, you would have a tragic end."

"Well, I wouldn't be marrying you, I just want to comfort you for an hour. I will promise you, that you will never be sorry. I can do things to you that you will remember for the rest of your life."

"That is probably true, but I have never been with a sporting woman. I'm surely not putting you down, but it is my religion that keeps me from doing that."

"What if I don't charge you. You would not be going with a sporting woman then.

"Please don't take this as an insult to you, because I think you are a good woman. However, you are in a trade where I could never be with you or anyone who has been at that trade. I think I have been with my last woman."

"Did you love her, dearly?"

"I did. She adored me which made me love her. I must confess, I loved two other women, also, who I loved as much. My first wife loved me so much that it saturated me until I was completely in love. She was killed by a bullet from an Indian while I was standing by her. She never knew what hit her.

My second wife loved me dearly and was blown up by dynamite that was intended for me, and my third was murdered by miners who misused her so much that they finally killed her to cover up their crime. I went back to the scene a couple of weeks ago and we found the miners, but no sign of my wife. Now you see why I would never bed you. I know you think you would give me great pleasure, but it would not be pleasure to me. I would see those three adoring women and it would ruin it even if I didn't follow my religion." Cheryl stood and said, "I can certainly see what they saw in you. I just wish I had met you ten years ago. I would have had a wonderful life."

"No, Cheryl, you would have died a terrible death. I'm glad that you never met me. I hope someday you can get out of this profession and find a good man that you adore. That is the key. If you can adore someone, it rubs off. I only loved my three wives after I saw they adored me."

Cheryl left and went back upstairs. She said, "He thinks you're dead. He went to where you were and found the miners dead. He searched for you, but thinks the miners killed you to cover up their crimes.

"You were right. He won't bed a whore and said he has bedded his last woman as he feels he is a jinx that causes their death. I tried to change his mind, but I could see I couldn't. I asked him if he loved his last wife and he said, 'dearly,' so you see he loves you. Why don't you change clothes and find out where he is staying and tell him you escaped."

"I've thought of that, but I would sooner or later meet one of my johns and that would ruin it. No, that part of my life is over, I won't ruin Alvin's life. He will get over this. He will meet another woman who adores him, as I and his other wives did. He will then marry her and live happily ever after."

"That is only in story books Cara. I do think if I met a good man, I would leave this profession. I know I could please him, because I have surely had the practice. I try to give my clients a ride they will never forget. I fake it like they are pleasing me greatly. It makes them finish quickly."

"Yes, there are things about this life that I like. I even get pleasure sometimes. It also pays well. I think in a year or so I can leave Fairbanks and go to a city in the lower states and find me a place. I might get a few girls and won't have to lie on my back except when I want to."

"Yeah, I have dreams like that too."

Alvin left the place where Cara worked and never dreamed she was one of the girls there.

That night he decided to return to San Francisco.

CHAPTER 18

STARTING ANEW

It took Alvin two weeks to get back to San Francisco. Getting transportation was his trouble. He was able to get a stagecoach to take him to Anchorage and then had to wait four days to get a ship to Victoria.

He was glad to be back. He visited Edgar's sister and deliver the bad news. He then visited Bob Melton. It was near lunchtime and Bob told him he was having lunch with Ivan Shulanski and invited him along. At the restaurant, Alvin told his story. They were both devastated upon hearing about the death of Cara and Edgar. Alvin said, "Only because they wanted me to die a horrible death did I survive. It turned out that I had incredible luck. However, my wife and colleagues didn't. I told Cara not to marry me, as my other wives met tragic deaths, but she said it was merely coincidences. I don't believe that now. I can see now, that I should have never married after Cuela. However, they both seemed to just fall into place. If ever a woman even looks at me again, I will ignore her." He had just said that when a woman walking by said, "Aren't you Mr. Alvin Scott?"

She was a beautiful woman with auburn hair and a terrific figure. Bob Melton said, "Yes he is, but he's undergoing temporary mental stress at this time. Can we help you?"

"Yes, I met him in Denver at his hotel. I am Lois Carne, the sister of Gene Carne, your partner. I was only seventeen then and had freckles all over my face."

Alvin looked closer and said, "Yes, I do remember you. I may not have, had you not had all those freckles. Where did they go?"

"They just went away when I grew older."

Bob said, "Won't you join us, Miss Carne?"

"I was suppose to meet my cousin here, but she hasn't shown up. Would you mind?"

Bob pulled out a chair for her and she sat down. The waiter came around and asked if they wanted a drink. All said, "No," but then Bob said, "How about you Miss Carne?"

"No, I'm not a drinker, but I would like some water."

The waiter turned to go when a striking lady in her mid twenties came in from outside trying to get her eyes accustom to the darkness. Lois saw her and said, "Millie, I'm over here."

Millie's eyes were now accustom to the darkness, as she came up to the table. The men all stood and she said, "My goodness, Lois, how did you discover all these handsome men?"

"Her eyes must not be accustom to the light yet," Bob said. They all laughed.

"Did you ever meet Gene's partner in the hotel, Millie? This is Mr. Scott, his partner."

"No, but I've heard about you. Where is your wife, Mr. Scott. Gene told me she was a beauty."

"She was killed some time ago by the Indians."

"I'm sorry, Mr. Scott. I'm sorry I brought it up."

Bob said, "Why don't you ladies have lunch with us?"

They both smiled and nodded. The waiter was there and they ordered. Both girls were good conversationalist, and Ivan and Bob were both glib. However, Alvin said nothing. He just ate.

Millie said, "Are you three partners?"

Bob said, "In a way we are. We help each other. Mr. Shulanski here is the best lawyer in these parts and I'm a banker. Alvin is our client as he is quite wealthy."

Lois said, "Hearing how wealthy your are Mr. Scott, Millie and I want to become dear, dear friends," and even Alvin laughed.

He said, "There is only one hitch to that. I have had three wives in last three years and each of them died tragic deaths. I am followed by the grim reaper, so if you want to stay alive, keep away from me, because those around me seem to die rather quickly."

Both girls gasped. Millie said, "What happened to them?"

"The first one was killed by Indian bullets, the second was blown up by dynamite, and the third was held and later killed by miners. Each death was worse than the last. So unless you want to die a terrible death, you will ride shy of me."

Both girls were in shock. Ivan then said. All those deaths happened in the wilds or mining towns. The last was on the Yukon river in Alaska. I think you will be safe here. Don't let it affect you. That all happened a long way from civilization like we have in San Francisco." Alvin said nothing. He just continued eating.

Bob then asked, "Where are you ladies staying?"

"At the Windsor." I am up from Denver to see Millie. She is a singer and an actress. She is playing at the Windsor, tonight." It was the same hotel that Alvin was staying in.

That night, Alvin went for supper, so he paid the head waiter to place him at a table in front. To his amazement, Millie was the main attraction. Her first song was Steven Foster's, *Beautiful Dreamer*. She followed that with *I dream of Jeanie with light brown hair*. Her voice was like honey. She came down to the audience as the orchestra played. As she sang she walked to Alvin's table and stood next to his table while she sang a romantic song without taking her eyes off of Alvin. The song told how she loved a man. After her singing, other acts were now being played.

Millie came to Alvin's table and said, "Do you mind if I join you?"

Alvin was now standing and pulled out a chair for her. She then said, "I know you don't want a relationship, but we can at least be friends. I have few, because I travel with the show. I'm going to be here another two weeks, so I thought we could do some things together and get to know one another."

"That sounds good to me. I like to be seen with a beautiful woman, and you are certainly that."

"Thank you, Mr. Scott. I will return the compliment as I find you a handsome man. It's not your outward appearance so much, but your inner self that I like. I had an instant like for you."

"I felt the same way, and I rarely do. It took me a week to even tolerate my first wife. She just grew on me. It took nearly a year before I saw her inner beauty as she was half Indian and I loathed Indians at the time.

"My second wife was the daughter of a sick woman who took me in, so that I could help her. Her husband had disappeared, and there was no one to do the man's work around the house. Her daughter was only nineteen and she at first didn't want any part of me, which was alright with me. However, that began to change until she wanted me. Her mother died, and if I were to stay in the cabin with her alone, I felt I should marry her. She wanted that, so we wed.

"On our wedding night her father showed up. He had been kidnapped by a greedy mine owner. That mine owner sent his men to kill him. I was away from the cabin bathing when they came and threw dynamite into the cabin and killed him and my new wife.

"My third wife and I came together quite incredibly. We were in a train wreck that nearly took our lives. We had to survive the harsh weather for a couple of days. We made it, but by then she was totally in love with me. I loved her, but surely wasn't ready to marry her. However, I could see she was completely devoted to me so we married.

"We went on a trip to Alaska. Another fellow, who was a naturalist, had planned a trip down the Yukon River. She wanted to go along, so I took her. During our trip we were attacked by four miners. One of them came onto my wife and I shot him in the leg. We left the miners, but they caught up with us and shot me in the leg, killed my partner and captured my wife. They had her for sometime, so you can imagine what they did to her. They killed her to cover up their crime.

"I miraculously survived, because a native family took pity on me. It took me a few months to recover, then I went after the miners. I found that they had killed each other, probably over my wife. I found their remains, but not my wife's. They had disposed of her body.

"After that, I decided to do without women as a partner as I felt I was jinxed. Everyone I get close to, dies a terrible death. I will be your friend, but if you want to live, don't get involved with me."

"I know you feel that, but I assure you, that at this moment in time, I have a career in show business that I have worked for all my life to get. I have had a few romances, but nothing too deep. I never felt I was in love. That said, I still like the touch of a man and his company."

"It looks like we will get along. I am much more drawn to you at this point in time than any of my past wives at this length of time. However, I must tell you, I loved my first wife more deeply than I could anyone else. She adored me and I her. Everything we did, we did together. Although we became very wealthy from a gold mine, she just wanted to be in the wilds with nature. I guess it was her upbringing as an Indian. I can still see her eyes when she looked at me. I think I miss that more than anything. When she looked at me, I could tell she adored me. You can't imagine how that made me feel. When I kissed my other wives, I was really kissing Cuela. I know it was wrong, but I couldn't help it. You can't imagine the love I felt when I kissed her, while kissing them. I've never told that to anyone, and I wonder why I told it to you."

"Because I make you feel the things you felt for Cuela. I understand your love for Cuela, although I have never had anything even near what you had. I felt it, as you were telling me. Even though vicariously, I liked it and had a wonderful feeling."

"Well, now you know everything about me. Tell me something about yourself?"

"I was born to two loving parents who raised me right. They taught me to follow my instincts. They taught me the value of a dollar and to always consider other people's feelings. The latter was the greatest gift.

"I wanted to be in show business since I was about ten. My folks took me to a show, where I fell in love with acting. I was gifted with a pretty fair voice, so I sang a lot. I auditioned with a company in Denver and they hired me. I was with them for two years before I was given a substantial part of this show and two years later, I was the headliner. I love show business, but it leaves little time for romance. I would like to marry someday, but I will not settle. I want a man I can love like your Cuela did. I want to be saturated with love with a man who is considerate and loves me like I love him. I will probably never find one, but as I said, I won't settle. I may become an old maid."

"You are a delight, Millie. I hope you find such a man."

They finished their dinner and Millie had another show to do. Alvin stayed for that show also and then walked her to her room as they were both staying at the same hotel.

When they arrived at the door, Millie said, "Would you kiss me goodnight?"

Alvin said, "That seems appropriate to conclude a marvelous evening."

They kissed and Millie kissed him like no other woman had ever kissed him. It was different, somehow. He felt different after the kiss. She smiled and said goodnight.

In his room Alvin told himself to watch it. Millie did something to him. He could feel her love when she kissed him, and wondered if she felt that way.

When Millie shut the door she leaned against it and caught her breath. Was she in love? She never felt like this before with a man. He did something to her that others had not. Maybe this was her man. She then remembered how his other wives had died. Did he really carry a jinx?

As she laid in bed that night, she was restless and couldn't sleep. Alvin had done a number on her. She didn't know how he did it, but he did. She loved him. Once she admitted that to herself she smiled and said out loud, "Nothing will come of it, even if I do love him."

She analyzed what he had said about his wives and concluded that he only loved his first wife. He had married the others because he was so considerate. What a man! No man was that considerate. She then wondered if he were kissing Cuela when he kissed her. She thought, *"I'll ask him."*

Alvin had been invited to have lunch with Bob Melton. Bob had brought a friend of his that was another banker. His name was Lester Prior. Lester said, "I'm having a party tonight at my house. My wife, Sandra, loves to entertain. Would you come?"

"That is very nice of you. Do you mind if I bring a friend?"

"Bring your friend, we will enjoy meeting her."

"She works late and we won't be there until after nine, is that okay?"

"It will be fine," Lester answered.

Alvin asked Millie if she could go with him to a party after nine that night. She said, "I can beg off for the late show. My understudy will be thrilled."

They arrived to find Lester's home a mansion. Millie said, "Well, he's a banker. I always wondered where my money went dealing with bankers, now I know."

They were introduced to a number of people. The last people they met were two doctors and a lovely woman. Their names were Doctor Roy Clark and Doctor Charles Wallace and his wife Susan.

Alvin asked, "My friend Bob Melton told me you are in a unique practice concerning the mind. Would you explain that to us?"

Roy said, "You know about the treatment of the body, well the mind has problems, also. Just to name a few, some people deal with anger, lust, envy and many other abstract nouns. Unless they are narcissistic, everyone has something about them that they would like to change. Doctor Wallace and I decided to try and heal these illnesses. We both agreed that this can be best done by someone who has some knowledge of how to treat them. We do it as a partnership with the patient. We tell them that they are now, not alone with their problem, as we'll share it with them, and together we can overcome it."

"That is very interesting," said Alvin. I have a problem myself that I would like to discuss with you. Would you take me as a patient?"

Roy smiled and said, "That is what we do. I see you as a very adjusted man, but all of us, even Dr. Wallace and myself, have things we would like to change or not be bothered with.

Dr. Wallace and I both agreed, that we get more out of this than any of our patients."

Susan said, "I particularly have benefited from their practice, and the best part is I'm not charged," and they all laughed.

She then said, "I will schedule you for next Wednesday afternoon if you would like."

"That will fit me nicely, Susan."

When they were alone, Millie said, "Why on earth do you want to see them about?"

"My jinx. I want to talk about it with a professional. Those men look like they can help me some, and I would like that."

"I see what you mean, Alvin. I'm glad you are seeing them. However, I saw the way that Susan looked at you. Stay away from her."

"My, are you becoming more than a friend?"

"It's the way you kissed me. It does something to me that no man has ever done."

"I'm glad you told me that, because I felt the same way. Your kisses are different than anyone I have ever kissed. I felt that way after our kiss."

"Well, you already have something to tell Dr. Clark," and they both laughed.

CHAPTER 19

A LOAD OFF HIS MIND

The appointment came and as Alvin entered the office, Susan came out from behind her desk and greeted him. She was wearing a nurse's uniform that made her look very sexy. It accentuated her marvelous figure and showed enough bosom that it would excite anyone. He thought to himself, *"I bet they have a lot of men clients."*

Roy greeted Alvin and said, "To get started, just tell me about yourself and your work."

"Well, I have no work. I was extremely lucky in discovering a gold mine that made me wealthy. So, I would like to tell you about my life from the time I was in the army up until today. It may take the entire hour to do that."

"I don't think so, Alvin. You would be surprised how quickly you can cover the years. Please remember, that I am your partner in this. We will shoulder your burden together, so you are no longer alone with it. It is now both of ours to deal with."

"I like that Doctor, I already feel some of the load is off me, now that we both are shouldering it. To begin with, I think I jinx people. I will tell you about my life, then you can analyze it, and maybe help me."

Alvin began and told in detail his life since he was ambushed by the Indians and Cuela saved him. It took only a half hour to tell his story.

After which Roy said, "I can see how you feel that way. I want to tell you that you told that story so vividly, that I felt the love Cuela gave you, and could see why you married the others. You have a very unique way of telling things. You would be marvelous doing my work.

"I feel you have had a marvelous life, despite the terrible tragedies. I would surely have liked to have known Cuela. I can also see why you think you created these people's death. You did by living the life you lived. However, I feel if I had lived your life and had done the same things you did, it would have produced the same results. I think most anyone would have, so it is not just you, it would be anyone. I think you wanted to blame someone, so you blamed yourself. Most people would. I feel if you stay away from dangerous places, you will live a normal life. Most people would agree that no person can actually jinx another. I do think the supernatural, meaning God, can change the course of a man's life. I, like many who are Christians, feel that God determines the length of a man's life."

"I suppose you're right, Doctor. It did me a lot of good to see you. You are a rational person, who has seen a lot of what goes on in the minds of men and women. I would think your job the most interesting work in the world."

That evening, Millie asked, "What did the doctor say, Alvin?"

"He said my thinking was skewed because of the tragedies, and I had to agree he was right. He explained that I was in some very dangerous places, and that nearly anyone who was there in the same circumstances, would have had the same results as happened. He then said the tragedies made me want to blame someone, so I blamed myself. He's right. I was so torn apart from what happened, that I wanted to blame myself. I now see he's right. That guy is a right smart feller. I wish I had gone into that practice."

"Then why don't you. You are still young, and have a lifetime before you. I can see what you mean about that being a very interesting occupation. Listening to other people tell what is keeping them unhappy would be a very rewarding occupation, especially if you could help them. I liked the way he said that he would be a partner of his patients and share their burden with them. I can see how that would really help, knowing someone was with you."

"If I did go into that business, I couldn't stay here. I would have to go some place else."

"How about Seattle. Our troupe has booked a month of performances in that area. Follow me up and let's continue being together. I am happier when you're around. You can start practicing Doctor Clark's trade by keeping me happy."

Alvin grinned and said, "I seem to be happier around you also, Millie. It doesn't matter where I live. I have no ties here other that Bob Melton and Ivan. I think I will go with you."

"Why don't you audition with our troupe. A couple of the men are dropping out."

"No, that takes some practice. If I were to go into acting, I would want to go to school and learn the nuances of acting.

My voice may be a problem, unless I could learn how to project it."

"I think that is a good idea. I will ask my manager if there is an academy in Seattle that teaches acting."

***

Cheryl came into Cara's room one morning and said, "Let's get out of Fairbanks. Most of our johns are dirty and awful. I don't want to be here any longer."

"Where would you like to go?"

"I was thinking, Seattle. People are more civilized down there. Most bathe. These men of the North seem opposed to bathing."

"Maybe you're right. A change of scenery would do us both good. This place has become stale. Let's tell Margie right now, that we will be leaving Monday."

They took a ship out of Anchorage and were in Seattle the next week. They found a nice hotel and then shopped around to find the best brothel in the city. They came upon a very nice place. It was owned by a bright lady, who knew her business. She could tell at once that these two were money makers.

Cara by this time had amassed over a thousand dollars. Her goal was ten thousand dollars, then she would quit this business and move someplace where people would never know her. She would claim to be a widow from Canada who just wanted to start a new life. She would pick someplace that had a lot of rich men. She would also visit vacation spas, where only rich people came. The new brothel only catered to the rich and both Cheryl and Cara were making double what they did in Fairbanks. Their cliental were older men, but much cleaner, and that pleased them both.

At night Cara still thought about Alvin. She knew she could never be with him again, but she still loved him. She again thought, *"I would have never guessed I would end up a whore. I'm glad mother and dad never knew. Alvin would be mortified. However, once I got used to it, it isn't so bad. I like to please men that way. I even get pleasure from it at times. I guess I was always oversexed."*

She then thought where she might go once she had her ten-thousand dollars. Back East would be the place. There are more rich people there, and no one would know her. However, if she ran into one of her johns, she would just move on. She might even try London. There would be no one who knew her over there.

Millie's troupe moved to Seattle. Alvin followed her. Even though they did not cohabitate, they did room next door to each other.

One morning when Millie was having rehearsal, Alvin thought that he would buy Millie a nice necklace. He asked the hotel clerk about a jewelry store, and he gave Alvin directions.

At about the same time, Cara wanted to have the clasp fixed on a necklace of hers and went to the same jewelry store. Cara arrived just before Alvin. There were a number of customers in the store. Just as Cara turned, she came face to face with Alvin.

He was stunned. He couldn't say a word. Cara then said, "Hello, Alvin. I bet you thought I was dead."

Alvin said, "Let's go someplace and talk."

They left and went two doors down to a coffee shop. Neither said a word until they were seated, then Cara said, "I was with those men for nearly four weeks. Baxter had died and that is why Mort came after us. He was alone, but he ambushed us. I thought you had died and I could do nothing about that.

"When Mort returned to the mine with me, he told Leo and Tim that I was his and they must pay to have me. This made Tim mad, so he calmly pulled his gun and killed Mort. I was horrified at how cold blooded he was. Both men used me in everyway that they wanted. I knew if I didn't comply, they would torture and kill me. So, I did what they wanted.

"Leo became enamored with me and I used this to try and get him to kill Tim. However, the reverse happened as Leo was not the killer that Tim was. I was then alone with Tim. He made me work in the mine. Everyday after work we cleaned up in a stream. He used me terribly. I bided my time and once he left a gun close to my hand when he was on me. I took it and shot him through the chest. He wasn't dead so I shot off his genitals. He then died.

"A few days later, I was at the river camp, and hailed a tug going to Fairbanks. I had only the money I took from Tim's pockets, which was just enough to get me by until I secured work. Having no skills I went to work in a brothel. I had picked up that skill when the miners had me, as they wanted sex in everyway you could think. I felt I wasn't worth anything to anybody by this time.

"I saved enough money to buy some nice clothes then changed jobs to the best brothel in town.

"I was in that brothel when I saw you sitting at the bar. I knew I could never go back to you, as I was now a whore. I was elated that you were alive. I thought you had no chance to live, as there are many wild beasts that I thought would kill you, as you were tied up.

"I asked my friend Cheryl to go talk to you. She said she would get you up to her room. I told her she couldn't. She bet me she could, which I knew was a cinch bet. You did give her some information that I dearly wanted to hear. After being with so many men, I decided you would be much better off without me, as we were bound to run into many of my johns, no matter where we went on the west coast.

"I am presently working in a brothel here in Seattle. It is now my chosen way of life. I still love you, but I am not in love with you. I finally realized that you married me because you knew how much I loved you at the time, and being such a gentleman, agreed to marry me.

"Please don't feel badly for me, because I have learned to like my profession. I feel I am doing a service for lonely and oversexed men. So you see, we could never be together again. Now tell me what has happened to you."

As Alvin heard her story he was shocked. He would have never believed that Cara could be a whore. However, as she talked, he realized anyone is susceptible to the dark side of life given the circumstances.

He then said, "I was very lucky. The day you left a native family came to the river to fish. I would have never made it without them. They were a loving family and I enjoyed being with them. The mother knew just how to mend me. I spent several months with the native family. I loved each on of them. While recuperating, they gave me a drug that eased the pain. However, it made me hallucinate. I had dreams, where I made love to all five of the women of that family.

"I came back to the river to find passage to either Fairbanks or Galena. I was able to retrieve my rifle as Mort had kicked it into the river. It landed in a small pool and I was able to recover it. He didn't search my pockets, so I had money as well as shells for my gun. I used the rifle to attract a tug going to Galena."

"That had to be a dream as I could never envision you making love to anyone you were not married to especially not a native woman."

"I hailed a tug going toward Galena, and stayed there until I could hire five armed men and a tug. We went back to that mining camp and found all four miners, but no trace of you. I thought they killed you to cover up their crime. I just knew you were dead, as I could see no way of you escaping from those men.

"I was so sorry what had happened to you. I felt I was responsible for your death. I vowed I would never have the company of a woman again. However, I met two doctors at a party in San Francisco, who deal with things of the mind. With all the guilt I had about all three of my wives, I wondered if those doctors could help me.

"Those men are wonderful. They taught me that given the circumstances, nearly anyone who was with my wives, would have done what I did and that I should not feel guilt about their deaths. After some hours of therapy, I realized they were right. I had just gone to places I should not have gone.

"I want you to go to these doctors. I know they can help you. Even if you decide to stay in your profession, it will help you. After what we have both gone through, I don't think we can ever get back what we once had. Our lives have changed too much.

"I am a wealthy man, Cara. I want to set up a trust for you that will pay you five-hundred a month the rest of your life. You can live anywhere you want, and enjoy a good life with that kind of money. Please except it and go to San Francisco and meet Doctors Clark and Wallace. Will you do that?"

"Only because you have asked. Like I told you, I still love you and will always obey anything you ask."

After setting up the trust fund with Bob Melton, he showed Cara how she could access the trust fund in any city. They parted, both feeling much better, particularly, Alvin. Just knowing Cara was alive and could get help, was a great burden off his shoulders.

CHAPTER 20

A NEW BEGINNING

Cara did go to San Francisco. She now felt she was free from being a whore. She asked Cheryl if she wanted to come with her, but Cheryl said, "No, this is the best brothel I could ever find. I have some regular customers now, and I don't want to leave that."

Knowing she had enough money to live quite well the rest of her life, Cara felt much better. She also was glad that Alvin felt okay about not being with her.

She arrived in San Francisco and knew she would be there for awhile so she rented an apartment near Dr. Clark's and Dr. Wallace's office. She had no idea how they could help her, but decided to tell them everything about herself. If they could rid her of the guilt she felt about servicing the miners and being a whore, she was all for it.

Doctor Wallace was the one she saw. She liked that, because Dr. Clark was young and she felt more comfortable with an older doctor. She began by telling him her whole life's story. She tried not to leave out anything, no matter how repugnant it was. She sometimes had to regress, when she remembered something that she hadn't mentioned.

The first time Dr. Wallace talked he said, "Cara, after hearing your life story, I feel most women would have taken the same path that you took. Some people in their pious ways would look down on you, but that is unrealistic. I see you have endured hardship in a realistic manner and I for one, commend you. You did the only thing you could do to stay alive.

"Many women look down on prostitution, but they themselves are one themselves if many ways. Women who marry for money may not feel they are, but they are. Women who cheat on their husbands are worse. Many these women are driven to other men because they cannot control the urges within themselves. I see you are burdened with these urges. Some people are given to alcohol and others to other vices. We all have urges that we wish weren't there. I see you as a very normal person, who did what she had to do.

"As far as Alvin is concerned, here again you did the prudent thing. His religious feeling and your past life, would have been a strain on a marriage that probably would end badly."

"I wouldn't take anything for the time I was with Alvin. He is the epitome of a good husband. I still long for his arms about me. He gave me the best love in the world, because I felt he loved me with all his heart. He may not have, but he made me feel that way. I know Cuela was his one true love, but I would take what I could get."

"You are one of the best patients I have ever treated. I think you can have a very productive life. I also feel you will meet someone who you will want to be with. Don't settle as many women do. If that man doesn't come along, you will still be happy.

"Where do you plan to live?"

"I want to go back to Philadelphia to see my parents. I haven't even written them, because I didn't feel I was worthy to be their daughter. You have changed all this in just the few visits. My burden is gone. I feel I can go on from here."

Cara left two days later for Philadelphia. Her parents were more than joyous in seeing her. She told them she was sorry she didn't write. She said, "The reason I didn't write was that I left Gerald Wilson. I know how our two families were close, but I ceased to love him and could not stay with him. I found another man and he loved me. But circumstances that I don't want to go into, came and we parted. We did part as friends, but we could no longer be together. That is when I decided to come home.

"I don't think I will stay in Philadelphia, but I wanted to see you and will promise to come on holidays."

Her mother said, "Just so we have you, Cara. We found out that your husband, Gerald, had done some unseemly things, and was not the man we thought he was. Your leaving him was what you should have done. We will never question you, as we know you are the best daughter in the world. We do hope you find someone to love, and Philadelphia is not the place. Just so we know where you are, and that you are safe and happy."

Cara left for New York City. She wanted to learn about the financial market and maybe be employed there. She would meet men in those circles, and went on vacation to spas where only the rich gathered. She was confident she would find someone to love her.

***

Alvin and Millie were in Seattle for four more weeks. The troupe was to go on to Victoria then.

Alvin said, "Why don't you quit the troupe. Let's go to Europe. I would like to see the sights with you."

"I will only go if you marry me. I need you at night. Don't you need a woman once in awhile?"

Alvin grinned and said, "Most of the time. I must tell you, I love to be with you and especially kiss you, but I still love Cuela and will forever."

"Can't you love two people?"

"Yes, I feel I can. Maybe you can get me to love you more that Cuela."

"I'll do my best."

Millie gave her notice and told the director that she may come back. He said, "Millie, I have a good friend in London who does essentially what I do. I would count it a favor if you will go see him. I will write a letter to him if you will agree to see him."

Millie said she would.

They decided to go by rail to New York and then on to London via a cruise ship. Eventually, they were in London. After a few days Millie called on Mr. Raymond Ester. He was directing a review at the Grand.

Ray said, "Thank you for coming. Tom said you were special, however, I had no idea you were such a beauty. Would you be so kind to sing something for me. I have a pianist available."

Millie agreed and she sang a favorite of both continents. After she concluded her song, Ray said, "Please sing next week in our review. I feel you would be cheating London, if you didn't."

Millie turned to Alvin and he said, "You can't cheat London, Millie," and grinned.

Millie sang and was a smashing hit. The reviews lauded her beautiful voice. Ray talked her into singing two nights a week (Friday and Saturday) while they were in London. They were in London six months. The traveled to Paris with Ray's troupe. They were there six months also.

She finally begged off and they went to Italy via Switzerland. They loved Switzerland so much, they stayed six months there. When it began to get cold they went on to Italy.

They were in Europe two years. Millie's reputation had followed her and she sang in all the places they stayed. However, after nearly three years they wanted to go home.

Alvin said, "So where is home?"

Millie said, "I loved Seattle."

"I did too. Let's go there for awhile, and if we want it be our permanent home, we can think about buying. or building a house there."

They had only been in Seattle a couple of weeks and Millie was asked to be in a musical show. She loved performing, so Alvin said, "Do what you love to do, Millie."

While Millie was rehearsing, Alvin needed a new coat, so he went shopping in a large department store. He was looking at the coats and another man was looking at them, also. They began talking and Alvin told him his name. The man just said, "Call me Frenchy, as everyone else does."

Alvin asked, "What do you do?"

"I have a trading post on the Yukon about halfway between Fairbanks and Galena."

Alvin was stunned. He said, "Did your trading post burn about six years ago."

"Why yes, how did you know that?"

"I was shot at that location and if it hadn't of been for a man named Naso, his wife Saleso and their children, I would have died."

"Naso told me about that. I hid out while that gang of cutthroats pillaged my place. A year later, I went back and rebuilt my trading post. I'm here in Seattle to line up supplies. I can buy them here and have them shipped to Fairbanks much cheaper than buying them in Alaska. There are also things I can't get in Alaska that I need."

"Let's have lunch together."

At lunch French said, "Do you know you fathered five children while you were there."

Again Alvin was stunned. He said, "I didn't father any children, Frenchy."

"You didn't know it, but Saleso drugged you so you would not know. But each of the women including, Saleso, slept with you."

Alvin then thought of the erotic dreams he had, and began to realize that what Frenchy was telling him was probably true. He then said, "Why would they do that, Frenchy?"

"Naso said they needed to make their family strong, so they all agreed that having you father the children would make their babies bigger and stronger. It was a matter of survival. I think you can see that they were isolated. They were shunned by the other tribes so Naso left and built that house. I helped him design it and ordered supplies to make it a fine house to live in.

"I hope you aren't overly upset. I think you did an admirable thing. Do you think you would like to see your children?"

"I surely would. I will go back with you, if you will let me."

"I would be honored, Alvin."

Alvin told Millie that he had met an old friend from Fairbanks and would like to go with him, as his friend needed him.

Millie said, "I'm so busy that I would rarely see you anyway, Alvin. Go and have fun. If I'm not here when you return, I will be in San Francisco. She gave him a schedule of the troupes gigs for the next six months.

They left two days later. They caught a ship to Anchorage and then a stage to Fairbanks. Frenchy had his own boat and they departed the day the goods arrived that Frenchy had purchased in Seattle.

As they traveled Alvin asked, "I suppose the babies are all about the same age. How will their mothers explain their relationship when they get older?"

"I suppose they will cross that bridge when the subject comes up."

"Do you think they will welcome me?"

"Of course. You're the father. Naso told me you were the best man he ever met. Soleso says the same, and the girls love you."

"I'm surprised that Naso encouraged Soleso to sleep with me."

"He thought it would help his family, and he will do anything to help their family."

"Do the girls ever see any other men?"

"No, but I think you can help that by encouraging men to come hunt in this area."

"I will surely do that. The Lord has blessed me financially and I think I can get men to come to their area. They will need a school teacher for sure. I will finance that. I can build a hunting lodge near Naso's house. However, I will have to talk that over with Naso before I make any plans."

They arrived and spent the first two days getting the supplies in place. Alvin then said, "I want to go to see Naso and his family."

Alvin remembered the way. As the weather was nice, he made the trip in one day. It was dusk when he arrived and he could see the lights burning in the windows. He knocked on the door and was met by Naso who embraced him at the door.

Soleso asked, "Who's at the door, Naso?"

Naso said, "The father of our family, Alvin Scott."

The girls all yelled and came to the door. Alvin was already inside and spent the next few minutes hugging everyone.

Naso said, "Did Frenchy tell you about the children?"

Alvin nodded with a smile and said, "May I see them."

With great pride each of the women showed the children and told Alvin each of their names. They were all about six years old and could speak some English. The combination of the two races made handsome children.

Alvin said, "It will take some time to learn their names. They can call me Alvin."

Soleso asked, "Are you hungry. Alvin?"

Alvin nodded and Soleso made him a place at the table, then brought him food. All the girls sat at the table smiling.

Alvin outlined his plan to bring a teacher and maybe some hunters to their area and thought it prudent to build a lodge to house them. He said, "The Lord has blessed me financially and I can accomplish these things."

Soleso said, "That would be nice. We need some men around and they can help store food for winter."

Alvin stayed a week and he and Naso planned the place for the lodge and another for a cookhouse. Alvin said, "If you have a cookhouse and all of the men and your family eat together it will bring you together more quickly."

Alvin left and returned to Frenchy's outpost. He outlined his plan for a lodge and cookhouse and Frenchy agreed that it may bring husbands for the girls. He also knew it would help his business, greatly.

In Fairbanks Alvin placed an ad in both the Anchorage and Fairbanks' papers for an elementary school teacher. He said the man must be single and under thirty. He placed another ad that said he was forming a fur company and needed three hunters to form the company.

He had two men answer the ad for the school teachers job and interviewed them. One was unencumbered, but the other was engaged, so the hiring was easy. The man's name was Melvin Smith, and he was a soft spoken man that said he liked to hunt and fish. He said the job was ideal for him.

Alvin said, "Melvin, you will be teaching some young ladies that are natives and their children. Teach them English first. Then teach them to read and write in English. This will be a task as none of them speak very much English. I'm sure you do not speak their language. Can you handle that?"

Melvin said, "Actually, not speaking their language will make it easier, because they must speak English to communicate. I have done this before and love it. You say there are four young women?" "Yes, and I will tell you what happened, so you will know the whole situation."

"I ask that you keep it to yourself as it is a bit sensitive." Alvin then told him what had happened and why.

Melvin smiled and said, "I can understand their motive and further see you were without fault. I will teach the children with their mothers, I will also teach the father and mother of the girls. This is a rare opportunity, and I relish the challenge."

Alvin then told about the hunters he was engaging. Melvin smiled and said, "I think you are trying to find husbands for these women."

"You've guessed my motive, but I also want them to be educated and especially the children."

"I can see you are a fine man, Alvin, and it will be a pleasure to work with you."

"Actually, Melvin, I won't stay as I have a wife." He then told about Millie and her career. Melvin had seen her perform and said, "My, you have a wonderfully talented wife, Alvin."

Four hunters were interviewed and all were in their thirties. Alvin liked them all and said, "I only wanted three of you, but after meeting you, I want to hire you all. This is a business and I expect to make money from."

In the meantime, Alvin sent two carpenters and a steam driven saw to the area and Frenchy helped plan the buildings. All had bathrooms and the cooking was handled by Soleso and the girls. Alvin had bought the girls and their children clothes that made them more comely.

After the first year, the fur company began to pay off, so Alvin raised the wages of the hunters. Alvin had also employed a man to drive a wagon between Frenchy's outpost and Naso's place. They took products that were needed in, and furs back to Frenchy. The business was good. He made Frenchy his partner and Frenchy ran the business end, so all prospered.

After the operation was successfully being run, Alvin felt he could go back to Seattle. Two of the girls had already married two of the hunters and it looked like all of them would be married, soon. Houses were now being constructed for the new families. Naso's settlement was becoming a small village.

Millie was glad to see him. He had been gone over a year and she was worried he might have grown tired of her. He quickly quelled that notion.

They were building a mansion overlooking Puget Sound, when Millie found she was pregnant. Millie quit the theater except for special events. They had another child a year later.

Once a year they would go to the settlement. Millie loved the trip and they decided to build their own house there and stay for the summer. She wanted their children to know Alvin's children by the native girls. They all spoke excellent English now. The school teacher married the youngest girl and the population grew.

One day Nasa was sitting with Alvin alone and he said, "You made my dreams come true, Alvin You are a true friend.

THE END

Printed in the United States
By Bookmasters